Totally Five Star:
Las Vegas

VEGAS SIN

JAMBREA JO JONES

Vegas Sin
ISBN # 978-1-78430-991-6
©Copyright Jambrea Jo Jones 2016
Cover Art by Posh Gosh ©Copyright January 2016
Interior text design by Claire Siemaszkiewicz
Pride Publishing

Published in 2016 by Pride Publishing, Newland House, The Point, Weaver Road, Lincoln, LN6 3QN, United Kingdom.

Pride Publishing is a subsidiary of Totally Entwined Group Limited.

VEGAS SIN

Dedication

I want to thank Karen Hatfield and Sarah Snider for the help in naming my story! Brainstorming with you guys was fun. Cinders, thank you for coming along to help too and Evil Will—your efforts were appreciated even if this isn't a BDSM story.

Thank you JP Barnaby for an interesting conversation on Facebook! Because of that a fun scene was added to this story that otherwise might not be there.

To Totally Entwined for always giving me the chance to grow and believing in me and thank you for the opportunity of working with my very first editor, Faith.

And to Joy.

Chapter One

Owen Carpenter strolled through the precinct like he hadn't a care in the world. He whistled some song that was on the radio before he shut the car off. Now it would be stuck in his head all day. He might as well share it with others. What could he say, he was a giver.

It helped the façade he put on for others and it drove his partner nuts when he did it, which was a plus. He always had the outward appearance of being calm and that everything was right in the world. He had to or he'd go batshit crazy and he couldn't have that. He was armed, after all, and it could be dangerous for a cop to go all mental. He needed to be focused, and if pushing his issues back helped, he'd do it all day. Owen tried to keep his private and work lives separate. That didn't always happen, because his partner liked to give him a hard time, which was why Owen did his best to drive Jeff crazy. Of course they were more like brothers than partners. Most days that was a good thing, especially when Jeff's wife sent in muffins for him. The best was when Sally came in and personally handed him some goody to make sure Owen got some. Jeff hated that and tried to steal his goodies, but Sally made sure Owen was taken care of.

This morning was one for the books, that was for sure. One of those days he wished he could do over. His sister and niece had been kicked out of their latest apartment the night before, so they were shacked up with him for the duration. He had to haul all their stuff to his place, and it was a mess. At least he had a garage to hold some of the stuff. Not that his sister was kicked out of her home every day, but Susan wasn't the best with her money on a good day. He tried to help the best he could, but she didn't always appreciate her big brother butting his nose into her business. At least Susan hadn't gone back to the booze. That would add a whole other set of issues he really didn't want to deal with. He'd helped get her dry once and hoped like hell it stuck because he didn't know if he could go through that again.

His niece, Gabbi, was a sweetheart, and he'd do anything for her. She was only nine and cute as a button with her long blonde hair and big blue eyes. Yeah, he might be wrapped around her little finger, but he didn't know if he'd ever do kids, so she might be all he ever had. He planned to spoil her as much as possible. When the time came, he'd make sure she was treated right by whoever she wanted to date. *If* he let her date. She was an old soul who acted more like Susan's mom on most occasions, which made him want to pamper Gabbi even more.

His own mom had trouble dealing with two new people in her space — when she remembered it was her space. The Alzheimer's was getting worse. It was hard enough most days when she didn't remember him, but now she kept asking who the two hussies were and why they were in her house. Gabbi didn't fully understand why her grandma couldn't remember her and called her names.

His mom was in the process of being moved to a new home this week because taking care of her was just too much. He hated the fact that she had to go, but it was past time. A nurse came by to sit with her while he worked. The only problem with that was that they didn't always send the same person and it got confusing for his mom. If she was in a home, she could get used to the same people. It would give her a bit of the stability she'd lost the last few years. At least with his sister at the house, he could get some help with their mom—not that Mother would remember either of them—but Susan needed to help out. Breakfast had been a disaster with his mom dumping her food on the floor and stomping out of the room like a cranky two year old. Poor Gabbi had had to do some clean up, because Susan had decided to sleep in, and he'd been running late for work. He made a note to take Gabbi to a movie or shopping for the weekend. If she really wanted to go, he'd take her, even if he hated going to the mall.

Now he needed coffee—stat. He hated the slop they had in the office, but it was better than nothing. He'd forgotten to set his coffeemaker up to brew last night. Of course, he'd been dealing with a sobbing sister and a too-serious niece. He hoped that nothing big had been tossed on his desk, but he wasn't sure he'd get that lucky. It had been a busy week—not that he should be surprised—since it was Vegas, after all. The lights and gambling attracted all kinds. It kept him busy most days. Owen had just wrapped up a case late yesterday. A domestic violence situation where the boyfriend had killed the girlfriend. It was pretty open and shut, but he'd still had to cross his T's and dot his I's so the guy didn't get off on a technicality.

At least he wasn't set to testify anytime soon. He hated going to court. He'd rather be solving cases. Some of the other guys looked at it like a day off, but not him. All those people staring at him while he did his best not to fidget in the seat.

His partner was out on leave so that left him picking up the slack. They had a few cases open that he'd have to take a look at and see what else he could do, as long as something new didn't take priority.

The coffeepot was almost empty. There probably wasn't even enough for a cup. It seemed the guys did that shit all the time. Owen poured the little bit into his cup. At least it would give him a jolt while he waited for a fresh batch to brew. He didn't even think about how long the pot had been setting there. The others would pass it up in a heartbeat and wait until someone else made it, then they would all jump on it like vultures. Shit. He really should have brewed some at home.

Maybe he would swing by a Starbucks later. He hated to spend the extra money, but he couldn't live without the nectar of the gods. The sludge in his cup wasn't going to cut it. After one sip, he dumped it out. Nothing was going to save that coffee. Leaving the pot brewing, he made his way to his desk. It was pretty quiet. The shift change meeting wouldn't happen for about an hour, so he had time to go through the files from yesterday.

Owen had just settled in when his captain threw a file on his desk. He knew he wouldn't be lucky enough to skate through the day with the files he already had. He'd jinxed himself.

"Kidnapping. This is the fifth one in as many weeks. They're all tall, blonde, mid- to late twenties. That's about the only thing they have in common. One is a local and the other four were all staying at different hotels. I want you and Polubinsky on this."

"He's on leave." Owen picked up the file.

"You can start on it. He'll catch up. Take a look at the notes and do some legwork. This one takes top priority for now. I want them found. None of them have shown up dead *yet*, and I'd like to keep it that way. There have been no demands or ransom calls. The first couple were filed and looked at briefly, but nothing came of it. When the third was reported, we noted a pattern. Now that we have five, we have to consider that they might be connected. None of the vics look like the types who would just walk off, but you never can tell. You know how it is. Most of them can be chalked up to having too much fun, but it's been weeks on the first two girls. The local lady has a kid and appears responsible. She has lived here in Vegas her whole life, so I don't see her running off now." The captain shrugged and left.

Owen flipped through the file. There wasn't much there, just a description of each girl and where they were from, the hotels where they had stayed. They were all over the place. One of the hotels caught his eye—Totally Five Star. He'd take a look at that one last. He had a friend who dealt cards there. Plus it was the place he loved to go once a month. He'd missed last month and it looked like he was going to miss this month too with all the stuff going on.

At least now he could get that cup of coffee he wanted. Plus he'd get out of the morning meetings, which could get boring, especially if Espinoza got to talking. It sucked that it had to take a foul-play case to get him out into the streets, but he'd take it.

It was only eight in the morning and it was already reaching the hundreds. One of the things he loved and hated about Vegas, but it was his city, so he dealt with it. He really couldn't imagine living anywhere else.

First stop for interviews would be to the local girl's family. It looked like she was the first one taken. He just hoped the leads hadn't run dry with that one. It sucked that sometimes it took a murder to find these people. Most of the time they turned up safe and sound. For some they just needed time away from the world. Hell, he could understand that. At times he wished he could run away, but he had too much responsibility and he wouldn't leave like that. It just wasn't in him to flee his duties.

Who would take care of his mom or his sister, not to mention Gabbi? If anyone needed him, it was the kid. He was the only one she could act her own age with.

* * * *

The drive to Jade Chase's house didn't take long. She lived pretty close to the station. He wondered where she had been when she was taken. Usually the cops were pretty heavy in this area.

The interviews could be a good thing or a bad thing. Owen hated that first look a person got when he showed them his badge. It was like their world crumbled right in front of him. He was going to talk to the victim's boyfriend. The first suspect was usually someone close and the notes showed he'd been questioned once already.

He braced himself after knocking on the door.

"Just a sec," someone called from inside.

The door opened to a plain-faced man with shaggy brown hair and brown eyes. Someone who would blend in. Owen noticed a little boy hiding behind the guy's leg.

"Can I help you?"

"I'm Detective Owen Carpenter. I—"

"Did you find my mommy?"

Owen crouched so he was eye level with the kid.

"I'm sorry—" Owen looked up at the boyfriend.

"Tommy."

"I'm sorry, Tommy, not yet. I need to ask you guys a few questions to help me find her. Would that be okay?"

Tommy's eyes filled with tears.

"Tommy, why don't you go upstairs? I'll talk to the detective. Okay?"

Owen stood. Man, he hated this part of being a cop. He was the guy who should be bringing hope to the victim's family, but here he was with no news at all. All he could do was his job and hope like hell he found this woman and returned her to her family. He just worried that it wouldn't happen. It had been about five weeks since Jade Chase had been reported missing. If she hadn't returned by now, she might not return at all, and he hoped he didn't have to come back and tell Tommy his mother was dead.

Chapter Two

Harrison Boone surveyed his domain, his hands on his hips and his jacket thrown back. His tie was askew, but his hair was neat, as if he'd just gotten ready for the day. It wouldn't stay that way for long, because he had a tendency to run his fingers through it, which was why he kept it so short. The Army might have influenced him some. He wasn't a teen with hair down to his shoulders anymore. He had responsibilities and liked to look the part, not to mention hair could be used in a down and dirty fight. Not that he got into many of those anymore. It was why he had employees under him. Of course, at the classy hotel he worked for, he didn't have to worry about many fights breaking out.

He lived and breathed the Totally Five Star Hotel. He'd stay there twenty-four-seven if he could, but he had a house off the strip. It wasn't much to look at, but it was his. Of course, he did have a cot in his office for those nights he couldn't make it home.

It was his job to make sure the guests were safe and sound. The casino could give him fits at times. People tried to count cards or cheat him, but he had a good staff under his belt, handpicked by him. Only the best for the Totally Five Star, and he was the best. Harrison was the head of security and took his job very seriously, having worked his way up from security guard to top dog. He looked throughout the control room. People pored over monitors, viewing the gambling area. It was a nice space with plenty of gaming tables. The casino scheme was done in deep reds and black with white accents. One of the best-looking ones on the strip, in his opinion. Tonight was a good night. Things were running smoothly. He was about to take a turn walking the floor when he spotted him. The man was of average height with sandy blond hair and a nice body. Harrison wished he could tell what color the man's eyes were, but the screens weren't *that* good. It was Vegas, not a Hollywood flick.

There was nothing amiss with the man, but something about him pulled at Harrison's attention. It had to be his resemblance to Ethan. God, how he missed his best friend. The nightmare from last night still echoed in his head. If he closed his eyes, he could see his friend falling down over and over again with a saturation of red blossoming on his chest, his stomach and finally his head, his helmet flying through the air. Harrison couldn't save him. He never did, not in real life or the dreams. He should have been able to save his best friend while he slept, to have that one hope, even if it wasn't when he was awake, but then it wouldn't be considered a nightmare if it had ended on a happy note instead of him waking up in a panicked sweat. Harrison shook the memories off. The ones of him crawling on his hands and knees through the desert floor, the sand kicking up as bullets flew around him. It wasn't the first time and wouldn't be the last he was forced to play that memory over in his head.

He'd seen the man in the casino before. It seemed like the guy came once a month or so and he never did much gambling. Not that Harrison paid that much attention. At least, that's what he told himself. Harrison didn't look into it too much because he'd feel like a stalker or something. It was bad enough he could pick him out of the hundreds of other people. He might have noticed because the guy always went to Drew's table, but nothing ever appeared amiss, and he'd check by having a guard walk by the table a few times. The guy was just enjoying a game with a favorite dealer. It wouldn't be the first nor probably the last time the stranger had shown up on his monitors. The guy never won big so it wasn't a concern—or it shouldn't be.

After one hand of poker, the guy was gone from the screen and Harrison could finally snap out of his daze. It was getting a bit ridiculous, if he were honest with himself. He wouldn't see the guy again until sometime next month. He could count on it and some days he did. That was how sad his life had gotten.

"Boss, you okay?"

He looked down at Raymond, one of the security guards on camera duty today. He was a quiet guy who was good at his job and stayed to himself a lot. Harrison usually saw him sitting by the fountain, eating lunch. He'd thought about joining him, but something told him Raymond enjoyed his time alone, so Harrison left Raymond to himself.

"I'm good." Harrison patted Raymond on the shoulder and left the security room.

It didn't stop him from thinking about the tall stranger. What he needed to do was get laid. That would take care of the problem. It had been a dry spell for him because he had gotten tired of the one-night stands. He was getting older and it was time to settle down instead of going on the hunt when he was horny. And that wasn't just his mother talking. Harrison felt the pull as well. Probably because all his friends had found partners and he was always the third or fifth wheel. While a quickie with a stranger would make him feel better in the moment, it was always the loneliness later that got to him. So what if he wanted a cuddle and someone who shared some of his interests?

Hell, he'd be the big four oh next year and what had he done with his life? The military didn't count. That seemed like a lifetime ago. Sure, he'd seen exotic places, but nothing spelled home like Vegas, the most beautiful city in all the world — at least at night when all the lights were lit and dreams could come true with a toss of the dice. People may talk about heat, but that had never bothered him. He loved the place and couldn't imagine living anywhere else.

Harrison nodded to some of the staff as he walked through the casino. It was a much better place than the one he'd grown up in. His mother had been a showgirl and he'd seen his fair share of places, none as classy as this one. It was as the name said — Totally Five Star. There wasn't a penny spared in looks or services. Beautiful black chandeliers hung in the gaming room, and the lobby held the intricate beaded gold ones. Carpets with hints of black brought it all together. Tables of dark, gleaming wood had been installed by the general manager only weeks ago. Some might think the whole thing was too dark, but the white helped brighten it up as well as all the lights. The hotel had been featured in a few magazines over the years, but with the old tables — they had a shoot set up soon to feature the upgrades.

He was proud to work here and sometimes he'd bring his mom in for a show. He should give her a call later.

It had been a few weeks and if he didn't call, she'd get on his case. They had a great relationship and he was lucky to have her in his life. It was just the two of them and they stuck together.

Thinking about his mom got him back on track. He had a casino to see to and he didn't need any distractions. The man would be trouble. He could feel it in his bones. He couldn't help it if he wanted to embrace the trouble and call it his own. He was allowed a flight of fancy once in a blue moon. Now it was time to get back to work.

It was a quiet night on the floor, but it was a weeknight. Even Vegas had its slow nights, at least in the casino. Once his rounds were done, he headed for his office. He had some paperwork that he'd been putting off long enough. Maybe it would help get his mind off the stranger. Next time, he might find himself asking Drew how well he knew the man.

Like he needed that kind of trouble. The other employees would find out and he would never hear the end of it. The security team were as bad as a group of older woman in a quilting circle. News like that would spread faster than he could stop it, so he would keep his curiosity to himself.

Harrison's mind drifted back to the stranger. He wondered how strong his hands were or how he'd taste. Would his hair be soft to the touch?

Yep, it was time to get laid. He'd have to hit up one of the bars on his night off. Which, if he counted right, would be the day after tomorrow. His hand just wasn't cutting it, and he'd get over the lonely feeling — or make himself. He missed someone else touching him. The human contact he got at work wasn't enough and he needed — something.

Eye on the prize.

The job called to him. He had paperwork to finish, new hires to look over. He'd done his rounds because he wouldn't ask any other security officer to do something he wouldn't do himself and that included taking walks in the vicinity of the gaming tables to make sure things were going smoothly. If it made him take longer on his paperwork, so be it. The hotel would always be there for him. He could count on his job and for now, that was what he would focus on. Not some blond-haired man he'd never met before.

Duty called.

* * * *

The next night, Harrison was fiddling with one of the screens that had been glitching. He might have to take it off rotation. Then he saw him. The same guy was back again. It was enough for him to take note of. It usually didn't happen. It was once a month. No more. Last month he'd noticed the lack of the gentleman on the casino floor, but never had he come in multiple days in a row.

Something was off. Harrison continued to look at the screen. The blond sat and was dealt a hand. Same as usual, but not. He watched it play out. Cards were discarded and new ones picked up. The game was over fast, but it didn't end with a wave and the hot guy walking away. The man pulled something out of his pocket and showed it to the dealer. Drew shook his head and said something. That was it. The exchange took a few minutes, then it was over.

Now he had a legitimate excuse to go talk to Drew. It was his job to notice patterns and things that disrupted them.

"Raymond, switch to screen two and change it to sector five until we can get this screen fixed. I'll be on the floor."

Harrison didn't even wait for a response. He was out the door and down on the floor in a matter of seconds. Drew had two players at his table. Harrison waited until they were done and had walked off.

"Hey, boss. I was going to come see you on my break."

"Does it have anything to do with the gentlemen who left before those two?" Harrison jerked his thumb in the direction of the casino entrance.

"Yeah, my pal, Owen. How'd you know?" Drew looked a bit puzzled.

Harrison raised an eyebrow and waited.

"Oh, duh, cameras. Anyway, he has a case he's working on—"

"Cop?" Harrison didn't know why, but he hadn't been expecting that.

"Homicide detective." Drew nodded.

"And he was here, why?"

This couldn't be good if Owen was flashing a picture to his employees. Harrison wondered why Owen hadn't contacted his office to begin with.

"Something about missing people. He had a picture of someone who has gone missing. Guess she stayed here. Told him to talk to security. Not sure if he will go right to you, but I'm sure you'll hear about it."

"Any reason I haven't already heard about it?"

"He said he doesn't think she was taken from the hotel, just that she was staying here so he was gonna get a feel for the place or something. I'm not sure. Want me to contact him?"

"You're sure she wasn't taken from here?"

"According to him, no. But he has a few other leads he was hunting down too."

"Why isn't this on the news?" Harrison didn't expect an answer.

"No idea, boss."

"All right. Thanks, Drew. I'll let you get back to work."

A few couples had come up to the table while they had been talking. Harrison gave them a nod and went back upstairs.

The plot thickened. He was going to meet this Owen one way or the other.

Chapter Three

Raymond looked around the warehouse with pride. Large dog cages lined the wall. The girls inside could scream all they liked and they did, but it didn't matter because no one could hear them out in the middle of the desert. He found he actually enjoyed the whimpers of fear coming from them. Raymond hadn't been expecting that. He thought it would all be very clinical. He would take them, do what he wanted and get his deeds in the paper. This was a new level for him and he liked it. Actually, he was getting off on it. Another unexpected side effect.

It was time to step up his game in his grand plan. There was no news on any of the kidnappings and there should have been. At least not that he'd been able to find. If taking the women off the street wouldn't do it, a murder sure would. He rubbed his hands together and licked his lips. He was ready for this next step.

He had to pick who he wanted to kill. If it should be the first one he took or if he should mix it up. He had seven women now, so it would be good to get rid of one, keep it an even number. Not that it really mattered.

Raymond could easily pick up another woman. There were tons of tall blonde women in their late twenties walking all over Vegas.

The how was the first thing he wanted to figure out, then he'd choose a girl. Raymond needed a pattern. Something that he could easily replicate down the road. And he wanted to keep the police on their toes without making it too difficult for them. They didn't seem to be very smart and it would be fun to watch them scramble. So far that hadn't happened. The disappointment of what seemed to be a failure had him stepping up his game.

Did he want to go all gruesome and hack the girls up? Should he do simple? Maybe a gunshot to the head would do it, but that was so common and wasn't really a signature. He wanted something with flair. Looking online didn't help much. He wasn't some psychotic killer. He didn't have a driving urge to kill. It was an end to a means. That was all. And if it was fun, so what? He deserved a little fun. Having to work a steady job sucked beyond all that was holy. This was his reward and he was taking it with both hands, fuck whoever didn't like it.

He wanted to calculate every step to make sure he was famous — well, his acts. Raymond would be happy if he could turn on the news and see what he'd done. *He* would know who was responsible, even if the police never did.

Jack the Ripper came to mind. Raymond wanted to be that big and have the case never really be solved. It was a little harder in today's world, but if anyone could do it, it was him. He was smart enough, no matter what his grandparents might say. He'd show them and secretly be happy that he'd gotten away with something.

Maybe he'd tell them what he'd done and give them both heart attacks. But not yet. He wasn't ready.

So what was he going to do? That was the big question. He needed a signature. Carving something in the bodies seemed too trite. Raymond had heard of a killer using a book as a guide so he didn't want to do that. No way would he be called a copycat.

I've got it. Perfect.

The idea almost jumped out at him. He had items from each woman he'd kidnapped. They all had identification of some sort. He would use that, but not when he killed them. No, each woman would have another woman's ID placed in their hands. It was perfect because it would be what he left behind *and* a clue that he did indeed have the other victims.

I'm so fucking smart. Take that!

The first step was completed. He had his theme. Now to figure out how he wanted to kill the woman. He'd keep it simple. Start slow. He could always build on it. They would say he was escalating, but it would be all part of his grand plan.

To switch it up a little, he wouldn't kill the first woman he snatched. Not yet. He'd save her for later, but he would use her ID on the girl he choose to kill. And to shake it up more, he wouldn't kill the first girl he'd grabbed second either. He wanted to keep them guessing, but tie it all together.

Raymond walked back and forth along the line of cages, thinking of a simple way to kill the woman. Something not too personal. He'd make the first few easy by drugging them. He knew it would be detected in their systems, but that was okay. He would drug the first two before he killed them. Make them unaware of what was happening. As he got the hang of taking a life, he'd let them know what was happening so they could feel their lives slipping away—all part of his escalation.

Which girl would he pick? Each of them scampered back away from the door of their cage. Like that would help them. They would all die, and he'd add more women to his collection. He'd read somewhere that one serial killer had murdered well over one hundred people. Well, the authorities proved only that many. It was entirely possible the guy had taken out more. Raymond didn't know if he wanted to go that far, but it was a possibility. Maybe he'd go for the world record.

It was a goal he could work on. He had time, but he had to kill his first victim before he got ahead of himself. He just hoped he could actually do it. Thinking about it and plotting it were different than actually doing the crime. Kidnapping had been the easy part. Women could be so dumb. Show them a little kindness and let it be known he had money and they were putty in his hands. They practically kidnapped themselves. He didn't think they would off themselves, though. That might be asking too much. He could force them to murder each other, but he was pretty sure there were movies about that.

After one more pass in front of the cages, he knew which one was going to die. Raymond left the part of the warehouse with the women and went to his makeshift lab, where he had the drugs he would need. The next time he fed the girls, he'd add drugs, but just to the woman who would die. The others needed to hear the sounds that came from his workroom. It would keep them on edge. He'd enjoy it as much as possible because he only had one first.

Chapter Four

Owen was frustrated and even that was an understatement. The case was going nowhere. Seven girls were gone. It was like they'd disappeared in a puff of smoke. But that wouldn't even be true because someone would have spotted the smoke. He had no idea how the perp was kidnapping the women. There was no ransom note or call. Nothing. One minute they were there, the next they weren't. It didn't matter if they were with a group or not. No one saw anything.

He was waiting on a warrant so he could go through some video footage from a few of the hotels. How were they going to catch the person with nothing to go on? Soon they were going to have to do a press conference to warn women to be careful. Of course, he had no idea what to warn them of. Was the perp a man or a woman? A group? Owen hated not knowing. He was getting irritable, which was unlike him. Even Jeff had mentioned it—well, yelled at him to get out of his face was more like it. Owen grinned. That was the best part of his day, making Jeff spit and sputter, his face going all red. The two of them didn't really go at it most of the time. He'd have to bring Jeff in a peace offering. It didn't help that their captain was all over their asses to find something, but they couldn't find what wasn't there.

He had to stop thinking about, if only for a little bit. Maybe that would help get his mind back on track. It was time for his monthly visit to the Totally Five Star. He'd missed last month's and had only gone in a couple times because of the case. He'd talked to his pal Drew, flashed a picture at him, but he didn't know anything. Not that Owen expected him to, but he'd had a sliver of hope. He'd also spoken to a security guard, but he really needed to have a one on one with the head of security. He'd schedule that meeting soon. Maybe after his massage, or not. Why ruin a relaxing day? He'd set it up tomorrow.

"Uncle Owen, where're you goin'?" Gabbi was on the couch in the living room, watching the Disney Channel.

It seemed like it was the only channel on anymore. Hell, more than once he'd caught himself watching the stupid channel when Gabbi wasn't even there. It was a sickness, and he knew it was a Disney conspiracy to take over the world, one brain cell at a time.

"Hey, sweetie, I'm going—"

"He's going to get pampered." Susan fluttered her lashes at him, her hands under her chin.

Good thing he loved his little sister.

"Pampered? Can I go?" Gabbi turned on the couch and got to her knees to look over the back of it.

"Not this time, honey. I only booked for me, but next time, I'll make sure you can come too. You guys'll be okay while I'm gone? I'm spending the night too."

"Yes, Owen, we're perfectly fine to be here on our own. I am a grown-up after all." Susan sighed and sat on the arm of the couch.

"I'd believe that if Gabbi said it." Owen winked at his niece.

Gabbi giggled and put her hands over her mouth.

"Very funny." Susan stood and pushed on his shoulder.

Owen grabbed her and put her in a headlock, giving her a noogie.

"Hey! Stop!" Susan wiggled around to get loose, but she was laughing.

He let her go, only to have her shove at him with both hands. He stumbled a bit and caught himself on the wall.

"My work here is done. Tomorrow I'm going to go see Mom. Want me to stop here and pick you guys up first?"

"Can we go to the mall after?" Gabbi clapped her hands together.

"For you? Yes." Owen smiled.

"I think...I'll just...you know...stay here." Susan fiddled with the bottom of her shirt.

Owen tugged Susan into the kitchen, leaving Gabbi to go back to whatever show she'd been watching.

"Listen, sis, she isn't getting any better. It sucks that most times she can't remember us, but she's our mom and the only one we have. We don't know how much time we have left with her."

"It's not like she'll know." Susan sniffed and wiped her hand under her nose.

"No, but, *we'll* know," Owen whispered softly.

"Okay. I'll go."

Owen tugged until Susan was in his arms. He squeezed her tightly. They really were all the other had left.

"Why don't you really start settling in? Put some of your things up—get it out of the garage. Tomorrow we'll take Gabbi to get a few posters to make the room hers. Just—stay here." He let her go then leaned against the wall.

"Owen—"

He held up a hand. "No. Listen. It'll help me out. The place is too big as it is. I've got the room for you guys to live here. Let this be your home base."

"I can take care of myself." Susan crossed her arms over her chest.

"I'm not saying you can't. I'm not giving you a free ride here. You're going to pull your weight. I was thinking about getting a roommate anyway. This way I don't have to worry about that."

"No, you weren't."

He wasn't, but Susan didn't need to know that.

"I was. So say, 'Yes, Owen,' and let me be on my way."

"Yes, Owen. But I *will* pay rent and you know... stuff."

"You'd better count on it." Owen smirked at her.

Since that was settled, he felt better not having to worry about where they might go or when he'd have to move them again. It was for the best, and it wasn't like he had a sex life to speak of. The house was almost paid for and he wouldn't take much from her. Only enough to make her feel like she was helping.

Maybe someday she'd meet someone and move out, but for now, he felt better knowing she was safe.

"Now that we have that settled, I'm off to the hotel."

"Enjoy."

"I plan to. Maybe next month all three of us can go." Susan patted his shoulder and left the room.

* * * *

It didn't take long to get to the hotel. He was ready to forget it all, if just for a few hours. His spa appointment wasn't until later that night. He'd already checked in and put his bag in his room before going down to the casino floor. He'd see if Drew was working. Play a hand of cards. Then maybe he'd take a swim. Cool off a bit before his massage.

Owen looked, and there was Drew. He strode to the table.

"Hey, Drew."

"Owen, my man. How's it hangin'?"

"Low and to the left," Owen laughed. "You ready to let me win?"

"Never!"

They usually started out their banter in the same way. Drew took it as a personal challenge to never let Owen win and most of the time he didn't. Gambling really wasn't his thing. He sucked at it, but it was nice to catch up with a high school friend. Even if it was only for the few minutes it took Owen to lose a bit of money. Never too much, because he hated just handing over hard-earned cash.

Too many cops liked to gamble and drink. He was not one of them. Never had been. Even being in Homicide hadn't driven him to drink. He'd seen what it did to his sister. Not that he wasn't down with a beer every now and again, but the hard stuff wasn't for him.

Tonight he might relax with a cold one in his spa tub before bed.

"You heard anything about the missing woman?" Owen settled into his high-back chair and scooted it closer to the table.

"Only from what you told me last time." Drew shrugged and began dealing the cards.

"I thought so, but figured I'd ask." Owen looked at what he had. It was a shit hand. If he didn't know better, he'd think Drew did it on purpose, but Owen knew his friend was a good dealer.

"The head of security came down after you left. Wanted to know what was going on." Drew finished dealing.

"What'd you tell him?" Owen tapped the table for another card.

"Not much to tell. Aren't you going to talk to him?"

Drew gave him a card and Owen busted. Drew took the cards and Owen's chips.

"Yeah, I'm going to see if I can talk to him tomorrow. Wanted to get tonight in first. I missed last month. I think the month before too. It was overdue. Need to get the case off my mind anyway." Owen put more chips out. He'd play a couple games tonight. He was enjoying talking to Drew, even if it was work-related.

"Dude. Then why are you asking about it?"

"You know how I am." Owen shrugged.

"Yes, I do, like a dog with a bone."

"You callin' me a dog, Drew?"

"You know it." Drew smirked.

They'd never had a thing. They weren't each other's type. Drew tended to like them slim and trim while Owen liked a big, tall man who he could feel safe with. Drew was more his size. While he liked his friend enough, there was no attraction there. It was probably why they'd stayed friends as long as they had.

"A bit slow tonight, isn't it?" Owen took a look around when he noticed a big, strapping guy headed their way.

If it had been a movie, it would have been in slow motion—Owen couldn't take his eyes off him. The man had short brown hair and a scruffy beard. He was tall—

at least taller than Owen and built solid. He had to drag his gaze away before he disgraced himself. Fuck, if he wasn't hard from one glance.

"It'll pick up later. Oh, hey, the head of security is coming over. You can talk to him."

The game was over and Owen was done letting his money go. The guy looked familiar... Was the head of security who he thought he was? No way he could be that lucky, but he was. Owen had seen the head of security a few months ago. Of course at the time, he hadn't known that. He'd watched as the suit walked with confidence through the casino part of the hotel. It had turned Owen on. He didn't think he'd see him again. What were the odds?

"Drew."

"Mr. Boone. This is my friend, Owen Carpenter. He's the one I told you about."

"Thanks, Drew." Mr. Boone dismissed Drew with only a glance.

It was badass and Owen could only stare at the exchange. He needed to move or — say something.

"That's Detective Owen Carpenter." Owen moved a bit away from the table and held out a hand.

Why he had to announce that, he didn't know. Drew had already told him he'd let the head of security know who he was. Normally he wasn't this stupid around men. It had to be those bright blue eyes.

"Well, Detective Owen Carpenter, I'm Harrison Boone. Please, call me Harrison." Harrison smiled at him.

It wasn't a 'Hey I'm talking to the village idiot smile' either. It was a Joey from *Friends* 'How you doin'?" kind of smile.

Owen's day just got better. Harrison was gay and if he wasn't, Owen's gaydar was broken. Harrison kept smiling at him. It wasn't broken.

"Please, call me Owen."

"Okay, Owen." Harrison winked.

The lust went both ways—he knew it. Maybe he could not only have a nice spa day, but get lucky too. He did have a hotel room all booked. If he were lucky, Harrison could get some kind of break. They could go up—have a little fun.

"I was going to call and talk to you tomorrow about a case I'm working on." He silently praised himself for not fidgeting. It was difficult enough thinking when his dick was getting hard.

"Yes, Drew said something about missing girls?"

"Right. We don't think they were taken from the hotel because there have been a few reported."

"You think they're connected." Harrison gestured for Owen to follow him.

"I have a room!" Owen blurted out.

Chapter Five

Harrison stopped in his tracks. He'd felt the vibe upon meeting Owen in person for the first time, but hadn't expected the man to blurt out about his room. Not that Harrison would complain. He'd been fantasizing about Owen for a long time now. So much so it almost felt like he was sleeping and would wake up at any minute. The first thing he'd noticed was Owen's eyes. They were green. Oh so green. And his short blond hair was lighter in person. He had a body for sin and Harrison wanted to lick every inch of it — as soon as possible.

Fuck, don't let this be a dream.

"Sorry...um...I just meant we could go up there to...ah...talk." Owen shoved his hands into his pockets and looked at Harrison as if he didn't know what was coming out of his mouth.

It was kind of cute and the blush spreading across his face was hot.

When Harrison had seen Owen walk up to Drew's table, he knew that he was going to meet him. He'd waited for a phone call or something, but found out that Owen had spoken to one of the guards instead of calling him direct. He didn't want to talk business. He wanted to rush Owen up to his room, right then and there. Throw him on the bed and spend the night fucking him. But he couldn't. Not right then. He had a job to do and he took that very seriously. He did have a break coming up. Harrison shouldn't even be contemplating it, because he knew once he got Owen up to that room, they wouldn't be leaving—job or no job—and that wasn't like him. But he was going to throw caution to the wind and go for it.

"Let's do this. I need to make my rounds and I have a break coming up in ten minutes. Why don't you give me your room number—?" Wait, they were going to talk business. About the missing girls. Why not ask Owen to his office?

He knew why. His dick hardening in his pants was proof of that, and Owen knew it too, if the fact that he kept looking at Harrison's crotch was anything to go by.

Harrison chanced a glance down Owen's body only to find him in the same condition. This wasn't about any case. This was going to be about two men having a sweaty good time.

"Sure. Yeah. We can—shit, we both know this is more than about missing girls. Tell me you're feeling it too. That you want to come up to my room so we can fuck each other's brains out." Owen put his hands in his pockets and rocked back on his heels.

Owen kept surprising him. Harrison wasn't expecting him to be so bold with all the blushing and stuttering, but he was happy it wasn't one sided.

"Once we get to your room, we'll both be naked in seconds. Does that answer your question?" Harrison licked his lips.

"Are you sure you need to do rounds?" Owen smirked at him.

"God, yes. Be naked when—"

Three hysterical women rushed up to him.

"Oh, my goodness! Please tell me you're security. *Please.*" The one in a red dress clutched his arm.

They were talking over one other, and he couldn't understand what was going on.

Harrison held up a hand, trying to get them to focus. "Please, one at a time. I *am* with security. What happened?" Good thing they were already off to the side so they wouldn't disturb the players.

One of the women stood straight and seemed to get herself under control. "Our friend. She was with us about an hour ago, but now she's gone. We've tried her cell phone and—" She couldn't hold it together anymore.

"Could she just need some alone time?" Harrison had seen it before, but wanted to be sure. After all, Owen had been asking about missing girls.

"Well...yeah, but she always answers her phone. Like—*always.* It's a thing. We all joke about it, but she's a doctor and on call a lot. Plus this is her party. She brought us all here. She wouldn't just *leave.*"

The woman in red's voice was getting higher and higher. Windows would be breaking soon if he didn't calm her down.

"When was the last time you tried to reach her on her cell?" Harrison wanted to keep them on track.

"Do you have a picture of your friend?" Owen moved beside Harrison.

He guessed they could put fun thoughts behind them right then and there. Now they were both on the job.

"Yes, I do. From tonight." The one clutching his arm pulled out her phone and scrolled through a few pictures before showing it to both him and Owen.

She was blonde and tall. Maybe in her late twenties. If he had to hazard a guess, he'd say twenty-six.

"And when did you say you saw her last?" Owen was now taking over.

Harrison didn't really mind. After all, Owen was on the police force if not on duty. He knew more about this kind of thing than Harrison did being a security guard. He might have been an MP in the Army, but MPs didn't run a lot of kidnapping cases.

"Are you security too?" Red asked Owen.

"No, ma'am, I'm Detective Carpenter with the Vegas Police Department." Owen flashed a grin.

"Oh, good — I mean great. You'll find her, right? Please say you will," the cell phone lady begged.

He really should get their names, but Owen was ahead of him. He'd pulled out a little notebook.

"Could I get you to send me that photo? I'm going to need it as well as your names so we can get started on this. You say you tried her cell phone? Could someone try it for me again?" Owen handed over one of his cards.

"I'm Roxy," the one in red replied. "She's Ginger." Roxy pointed to the one Harrison had been calling Cell Phone in his head. "And she's Paula. We've been trying to reach her for over an hour. Stella is in the suite in case she comes back. I'm getting really worried. It isn't like her *at all*." Roxy took her phone out and made the call Owen had requested. "Still no answer. I've left messages too. Nothing. Sorry, I should probably tell you her name as well. I didn't give it to you yet, did I? I'm so scattered and very, very scared. Her name is Dr. Molli Harper." Roxy put her phone back in her bag.

"Okay, this is what will happen. I'm going to get your information. I want the three of you to head back up to the room. I'll call if we find anything. I'll walk the perimeter of the hotel and the grounds to see if I can find her, but I gotta say, it's easy to get lost here in Vegas. There is a good chance she'll show up in the room later. If that happens, please give me a call. I'll report back to the station and get my partner on this as well. Right now there isn't anything you can do."

"I'm really afraid. All kinds of bad things could happen. I watch the news. I don't want her to be dead." Ginger started to sob.

It took a couple minutes, but it seemed as if Owen got the information he needed. One of the women texted him the picture and he seemed satisfied enough to let them leave. Harrison was very impressed with Owen's professional side.

"We'll call you if she comes back. Please let us know if you find anything, Detective." Roxy led the others away toward the elevators.

"Shit, this is bad," Owen whispered as he watched the women walk away. He ran a hand down his face and suddenly seemed weary. The spark from earlier was all but gone.

Not that he blamed Owen. Harrison's own hard-on had disappeared the second the crying woman approached them.

"Why?" Harrison figured people disappeared all the time.

"Because she fits the description of the other seven women who are missing."

"Seven?" Harrison looked over at Owen with his eyebrows raised.

"Yes, but you didn't hear that from me. It isn't out to the public yet, but I have a feeling we're going to be announcing it soon. Take a walk with me?" Owen was all business now.

"Where are we headed?"

"You said you had rounds. I figured I'd go with you, keep my eyes open. Maybe we can walk the outside perimeter as well, flash the girl's picture around. I need to call my partner, get him started on the paperwork so it gets in the system and put this new woman in with the others. This is the second person who has stayed at the Totally Five Star who has gone missing."

"What does that mean?" Harrison knew it wasn't good, but he trusted the people at the Totally Five Star. It had to be an outside source. He double and triple checked employees' records. He wouldn't put his hotel in jeopardy.

"Nothing yet, but it could be the start of some sort of pattern. I'm hoping a judge will grant me a warrant to go over some video feed." Owen was looking everywhere, not really focusing on anything and just searching as if he could find the girl in the crowd.

"You don't need one for here. I'll cooperate." He wanted to keep the name of the hotel out of the news. No one would want to stay if they thought people were disappearing from the hotel.

"Great. How about we do your rounds and a bit extra then take a peek at your feeds. Maybe we'll find something." Finally Owen looked at him. He even managed a smile.

Harrison smiled back. He still wanted to finish what was promised. Of course things had to go on the back burner for now—he was a professional after all—but that didn't mean they couldn't play later.

"And after?" Harrison ran his hand down Owen's arm.

"Well, I have a massage that I need to cancel, but after your shift?"

Now Owen's full attention was back on Harrison.

It was a heady experience, being the center of all that lust. It rolled off Owen in waves and he wanted nothing more than to rub their bodies together. Naked. But — later. Search first.

"You still need to give me your room number."

Owen took his cell out of his pocket and dialed a number.

"Hello, this is Owen Carpenter from room five oh six, I need to cancel my massage. Yes. Okay. Next time. Thank you." The whole time Owen looked him in the eye.

God, it was going to be fun messing with Owen. He seemed smart and funny. More than just a good lay. Well, he *hoped* it was good. From their byplay he was sure it would be fantastic. He couldn't wait to get his hands on his soon-to-be lover.

"Nicely played, Detective Carpenter, nicely played. Let's start back by the outside wall of the casino and work our way to the door. We'll ask at the front desk, the gift shop and even the spa if they've seen Molli. Show them her picture. Then we can go outside and walk the perimeter. Sound good to you?"

"Are you sure *you* aren't a cop?" Owen smiled at him.

"I was an MP in the Army, but I have to say I've never worked a kidnapping. Mostly I broke up fights between hot-headed men and women blowing off steam."

"Why security?" Owen searched the room, never looking in one place long.

If Harrison had been in the security office, he would suspect something was up the way Owen never settled on one place. Harrison did the same as he gazed around the room, hoping to see the missing girl. Harrison wanted her to be lost in the crowd or getting a massage to help with the stress of getting married, anything but kidnapped from his hotel.

"It fit. I was done with the military. I have a bum knee with shrapnel in it, so I wouldn't have passed any tests to get on the force. Security is the best of both worlds. Worked my way up and I'm happy here. Why did you join the force?"

They were about halfway through the search and ready to round the corner headed to the entrance of the casino. So far no luck. He knew in his heart they wouldn't find her here, but he was still hoping for a miracle.

"Following in my father's footsteps. And my grandfather's, my great-grandfather's. You get the picture." Owen laughed. "I wasn't sure if I would join the force, but after my dad was killed in a shootout, I knew I had to follow tradition. I wanted to do something in the criminal system, but I was thinking more along the lines of a lawyer. Anyway, when he died, I had to help support the family. The plan was military to help pay for school, but I couldn't go away after he died. Sorry, too much information too soon?"

"No. Not at all. I asked," Harrison said, taking a second to squeeze Owen's arm.

He was liking Owen more and more as the night progressed. Harrison was almost happy they had this time to get to know each other before they slept together. It sucked that it was at the expense of a young woman, but that was out of his control.

"Yeah, it was a long time ago and I'm happy working where I am."

They continued their walk until they reached the entrance of the casino. It was going to be a long night.

Chapter Six

Raymond was beginning to think the Vegas police force was made up of idiots. He dragged the girl to his van and dumped her inside. She'd been chloroformed so she wouldn't put up a fight. To most people it just looked like she was drunk. It suited his purpose. He wore a cap and kept the bill low on his face so the shadows would hide him. He didn't run or even walk fast. He was in his element and no one would catch him.

The only problem was that he'd had to resort to taking her from the Totally Five Star. He hadn't wanted to, but he'd seen an opportunity to pick up a new girl. It only made it better that the detective was at the hotel that night. Raymond wanted to flaunt his skills. He had taken someone right under the police force's nose and there was nothing they could do about it. They would have to report on it this time. That was if the cop could take his eyes off Raymond's boss. He might have to take a person right in front of someone to get the attention he deserved.

Plus, they hadn't found the body he'd dumped yesterday. He might have to make an anonymous call to get the ball rolling before the animal life and desert heat took care of the girl. There was no way he wanted all of his plans ruined because some dumb cops didn't do a patrol on an area they were supposed to. And now Raymond was taking a few chances, but he knew where the blind spots were.

That was the upside of working in security at the hotel, not that he'd tell his grandparents the real reason he got into security. He would take all the women from Totally Five Star, but felt that would lead to him sooner than he wanted it to. The authorities might start suspecting someone inside the hotel. It was best to spread his crime throughout the city. Raymond had a contingency plan if they ever did figure out it was him, but he wasn't too worried about the need to run because it didn't look like the police had anything.

The great thing about coming from money was knowing where all the nonextradition countries were. He'd done his research long before starting in on his grand plan. Maybe he'd retire early after he made a name for himself. He already had a place set up in Dubai for when he was ready. It was kind of like Vegas and he could have his fun there too.

It wasn't like he was getting a taste for kidnapping. And it wasn't a sexual thing. Sure he got hard at the thought of hurting people and having power over them, but he had no plans of sexually assaulting them. That was taking it too far. Sex had never really been fun for him. He was fine without. If he needed relief, his hand was good enough.

When he'd killed the first girl, he'd made sure that nothing would point to him being a sexual predator. He did have *some* standards. Murder, now that was a shining example of evil. To hold the power of someone's life in your hands, to be a god among men — that was something to be proud of.

Raymond turned on the radio. The girl in the back was starting to stir, and he wanted to drown out any sounds she might make. The van was soundproof, so he didn't worry about anyone outside hearing. The blonde wouldn't be fully awake until they hit the warehouse. It was a longish drive, but he could do it in his sleep now. He made sure to take a slightly different route when he could. Not that he was under any delusions that they would be after him any time soon. He was the guy who was okay at his job. He never went out of his way to get noticed. His boss wasn't too bad, but man, he was an anal-retentive ass when it came to making sure everything was squared away.

Must be his military background, but to walk the floor every hour? They had the cameras, so why did they need to patrol the area too? It made no sense to Raymond. If he were running the place, things would be a little different, but he had no plans of trying to get noticed and move up the chain.

He had better things to do. Vegging out in front of a monitor wasn't so bad, but following orders sucked. He was his own man. Hadn't his grandparents drilled that into his head? He just didn't understand how being his own man translated to having a steady job.

No matter. He was on a new path now. One that would take him far and be more satisfying than anything else had in his life. The thrill and power he'd felt when he'd killed that girl was like no other high he'd ever experienced. He was ready to go again, but wanted to at least wait for the first body to be discovered. He did need to escalate the kidnapping if he wanted to scare the public into doing something.

Raymond wanted a public outcry that he was the cause of — the feeling of power would be tenfold.

The only thing that could make him happier would be for his grandparents to die and give him all their money. Not that it would stop the path he was on now. There would be more death before he was done.

The building was coming up on his left. He drove around to the back, just in case someone happened to be out there. There wasn't much traffic on the way, not that he expected there to be. It was why he loved the spot.

A moan from the back made him smile. It was showtime. The girl would be awake for the entrance to her cage. Raymond liked to hear them scream. They held on to hope for a rescue that would never happen. They were all going to die.

Chapter Seven

Owen opened the door to his hotel room and walked inside. The first thing he did was take off his shoes and let his feet sink into the thick, plush carpet. He wiggled his toes and enjoyed the soft feel against his feet. It was just as decadent as he remembered. The room had a wall of windows looking out over the strip, the lights bright and pretty, lighting up the whole space, making it feel magical. He loved keeping the blinds open and the lights off. It was romantic and made him wistful.

The room itself was a dark gray with black and red accents, kind of a carryover from the casino. Owen went to the windows and looked out, taking a moment to just breathe before he turned to really look at the room. Even the paintings were otherworldly. Owen didn't know much about art, but he knew what he liked and what the Totally Five Star had on the walls were pieces with bright bold strokes. He thought they might be called abstract, but he wasn't completely sure.

One time he'd even gone for a suite and they'd had complimentary champagne. He didn't know of any other hotel that did something so nice for its guests. The strawberries were a nice touch too. If he'd known he would have a man up there, he would have swung for a suite.

The great thing about the room he was in was the king-size bed, a thing of beauty. It was up on a dais and looked like it was floating on air—again with the magical feel to the room. His bag was still at the end of the bed where he'd thrown it before heading to the casino. He'd planned to move it after his massage, but things hadn't gone as planned. Nope. He had to catch a kidnapping on his day off and had missed his downtime. At least this time he'd managed to actually get *to* the hotel before work showed up to ruin it.

It wasn't like his job was a nine-to-five thing. It was one of the reasons he was single. Guys didn't want to date a cop who could be called out to a scene in the middle of the night. He wiped a hand down his face. He was tired—to the bone tired. It had been a while since he and Jeff had caught a case this big. Usually it was a few days and the case would be done. Not this time. Fuck, they needed to find the person behind all this. They were lucky that a body hadn't turned up yet. Where was the kidnapper keeping these girls?

That reminded him of the call he needed to make. He threw the package from the gift shop onto the bed and dug his cell phone out of his pocket.

The phone rang a few times before voicemail picked up. Jeff had probably forgotten to charge it again. Their chief was always getting on him about that.

"Jeff—charge your damn phone. You won't get this until the morning, but we caught a case, another kidnapping. It was here at the Totally Five Star. I've got notes and will get with you in the morning. This is the second person who was staying at this particular hotel who has gone missing, but I think this one might be the first one he's taken from the actual hotel. Maybe we'll catch a break. We need to report to the chief because this seems to be escalating. This is the eighth woman and it has been going on for over two months now. I think this calls for a public announcement. Fuck. What we really need to do is catch this asshole before we end up finding dead bodies. When you get in, could you pull all of our files? I'm thinking there needs to be a task force set up on this one. See you in the morning."

Owen pressed the end button and tossed the phone onto the dresser. Today was supposed to be all about relaxing, but it had been anything but that. After he and Harrison had walked through the inside of the hotel trying to find the girl, they'd moved to the outside perimeter. Nothing. The girl was not at the hotel. Owen had called it in so a patrol car would still be searching and Harrison had talked to the control room to make sure the people working were on alert.

There wasn't anything he could do right now. All the bases were covered and it was late. As much as he hated the fact that he wasn't poring over paperwork and canvassing the scene, he knew he had to take a break. They had no idea where the doctor had been taken from. They'd gone over tapes, but she'd just disappeared. There was a blind spot in the hotel that Harrison planned on taking care of.

Owen had been working almost nonstop for over month. All of it full of dead ends. He didn't want to go back to that little boy, Tommy, and tell him his mom had been murdered. They had to solve this case before someone was killed, but it had been too long. Every day he waited for the call saying a corpse was found in the desert. They had enough of that with the transients that walked away—wanting to lose themselves only to die of dehydration. The Vegas desert wasn't something to mess with.

He had to get his head out of the game. For at least the rest of the night. The upside was Harrison should be getting off shift soon and he'd be at the hotel door before Owen knew it. The chemistry between them was off the charts. He couldn't wait to get the security chief naked in that bed. He wouldn't be able to think with Harrison's cock up his ass. That was his hope anyway.

With those thoughts at the forefront of his mind, he tossed his duffel off the bed toward the closet. He didn't make it, so he pushed it out of the way. Owen dumped out the bag he'd gotten from the gift shop. The condoms and lube spilled onto the deep red bedspread. He threw the bag away and headed for the bathroom. He'd be nice and ready when Harrison showed up.

What he wouldn't do for this bathroom to be in his house. It had a nice big shower with glass doors and a bench inside it. The counter was one of those two sink deals — a his and hers. It was big enough that it also had a sauna-style bathtub.

He dropped his clothes on the floor and pushed shoes and all under the sink. Owen opened the glass door and started the water — something nice and hot to soothe his tight muscles. He took a moment to let the water cascade down his body before he began to prep himself for a night of hot sex. God, he couldn't wait. He was getting hard thinking about what was going to happen in just a few minutes, but he didn't want to touch his dick because he'd come and there was no way he'd be spilling his seed until Harrison was so far up his ass he could feel it tomorrow.

It really had been too long and the thoughts of getting himself off so he could last longer flitted through his head. Fuck. He could be strong and wait.

Owen unwrapped the soap and sudsed up his body, taking special care with his pits and crotch before hitting his ass. He soaped up his finger and used it to caress his own pucker. Owen leaned his arm against the shower wall to get some leverage. He lifted a foot onto the bench. He wiggled in one finger up to the knuckle and made painstaking care not to touch his prostate or he would go off before Harrison got there, no question about it. He added a second finger, then a third. It was a tight fit, but the burn helped ease off his orgasm.

He was as ready as he was going to be. All he needed now was Harrison. Owen shut off the cooling water before grabbing a folded towel off the rack. If he had thought about it, he would have turned on the towel warmer before getting into the shower. The Totally Five star had the best towels. They were big and soft. He had to stop himself each time from taking a few home. Maybe he'd ask Harrison where they bought them. Well—later, much later. They had other things to do once Harrison arrived. He'd just finished drying off when there was a knock on the door.

The knock he'd been waiting for.

His cock jerked at the sound, because Owen knew what was about to happen. Owen wrapped the towel around his waist and headed for the door. And there Harrison was all nice and put together in his suit. Owen wanted to know what lay beneath and hoped he wasn't drooling over the images that came to mind. Harrison had scruff on his face and Owen couldn't wait to feel it on his body.

Owen took a closer look at Harrison. Despite the smile on Harrison's face, he seemed tired.

"Hey," Harrison said.

"Hey yourself." Owen leaned against the doorframe and gestured for Harrison to come in.

"My people are keeping watch. They know to call me if they see the doctor who was taken. I made sure they had her picture." Harrison walked into the room, tugging on his tie until it was loose enough to pull it over his head.

Owen held out a hand for the tie so he could put it on the dresser.

"Thank you. Hopefully we get a call that she's been found, but I doubt it. Not with the way this case has been going." Owen leaned against the dresser then crossed his arms over his chest and looked his fill of Harrison.

"That stuff doesn't happen at the Totally Five Star. Not on my watch. I'll help any way I can. The first thing I'm going to do is get that damn dead spot covered with a camera." Harrison ran a hand through his hair. He looked as frustrated as Owen felt.

"Could you keep it on the down-low?" Owen hated to ask, but he wanted to cover all of his bases. He really shouldn't be thinking of messing around with Harrison. The guy should be a suspect, but he wasn't in Owen's mind. He'd already cleared Harrison. He would have to be a great actor if he was involved. He'd been too invested in finding the missing doctor.

"You think one of my people could be responsible?" Harrison stood up straighter, his spin stiff.

"I really don't know and could be grasping at straws, but something has to break before we get notified that one of these women is dead." Owen began to pace the room.

"I usually put a work order in for maintenance to replace or fix the cameras. I'll go with an outside company. I won't say anything, but the hotel has people here twenty-four hours a day. Someone is going to see a repairman putting up a new camera."

"They might, but maybe we'll get lucky. Hopefully it isn't someone from here. It just seems odd that this hotel was hit twice. None of the other places have been hit more than once and there are still hotels along the strip that we haven't had reports from. Maybe the Totally Five Star and the other six hotels are his playground. Really? I've got nothing. We don't have a crime scene for any of these. I'm just—"

"Exhausted." Harrison stood in front of Owen and put his hands on his shoulders.

Just the touch was enough to make Owen start to think of something other than the kidnappings. He should feel guilty, but he'd been working nonstop on this case on top of getting his sister settled and visiting his mom. Right now he needed to take care of himself and decompress. Maybe clear his head a little.

A night of hot sex could help him do just that. Harrison ran his hands down Owen's arms. Owen stepped closer, no space between them. The lust was strong and he was going to take full advantage of that, tired or not.

He let the towel drop to the floor, ignoring the soft swish as it hit the carpet. He only had eyes for Harrison. He had to look up. He hadn't realized earlier just how much height Harrison had on him.

"I think we both are. Time to recharge, and I don't know about you, but I think a nice romp in the sack with a hot guy is the ticket."

Harrison wrapped his arms around Owen. Now things were going the way Owen wanted. Some mindless sex to take his mind off life for just a small space of time was what he needed. Would it help him find the missing women? No, but it would release some of the stress.

"I have no problem being your hot guy, but I'm a little overdressed for the occasion." Harrison winked before kissing Owen's cheek.

"I totally agree." Owen slipped Harrison's jacket off his shoulders then placed it on a chair so it wouldn't wrinkle.

The tiny buttons were a bit much for his fingers. Harrison took over and had his shirt off in no time. Owen took advantage and ran his fingers through Harrison's chest hair. It was fuzzy and he liked it, so different from his own body.

He kissed Harrison's chest, flicking his tongue against a nipple. Harrison's moan was heaven. Owen wanted to taste the man's sounds. He pushed at Harrison's shirt, getting it completely off him, letting it drop to the floor. He pulled Harrison down to him so he could reach his lips. He liked the fact that Harrison was bigger than he was. He wanted to crawl up the guy's body and never leave.

Owen shivered, not from the cold, but from the fact that he was about to get laid. He hadn't felt like this in a long time.

Chapter Eight

Harrison let Owen drag his face down so their lips could brush together. It was a moment he'd waited for and it was worth it. Their bodies were pressed against each other's, but there still wasn't enough skin on his part. He reached between them to struggle with his pants, but his zipper wasn't cooperating because he was too focused on the kiss. He opened his mouth to let Owen in, their tongues dueling for dominance. Harrison forgot about his struggle and cupped Owen's head. He couldn't get enough.

Owen pushed at Harrison's pants and he wiggled his hips to help. Owen had finally loosened them enough they fell to the ground. Harrison went to step out of them, but they'd forgotten his shoes. He fell into Owen, pushing him against the wall.

They needed to slow down a bit or one of them was going to get hurt.

"Let...me..." Harrison backed away and slipped off his shoes before taking off his pants and boxer briefs.

Owen took his clothes from him and put them with the rest. He dragged air into his lungs as he struggled for air and Harrison was right there with him.

"Get on the bed." Owen stroked his cock with one hand and pointed with the other.

Harrison didn't even bother to argue. He was just as anxious to get started as Owen was. He moved the short distance and made his way toward the headboard. He propped himself up as Owen made his way toward him. It was sexy as hell and he would be in that ass soon. He brushed against a paper sack. He picked it up, taking his eyes off Owen for only a second to see what was in the bag. He smiled and looked up at the sexy man coming his way. Harrison hadn't even thought of getting lube and condoms. It was a good thing someone was being responsible.

"I'm going to ride you, Harrison, and if we can get it up again, later you can ride me, if you want. I'm up for anything, but this first time I want to feel your fat dick up my ass. It's been too long."

Harrison licked his lips. His night just got better. Any tiredness he'd felt evaporated with thoughts of sex and Owen.

"I'm game. Get that sweet ass over here." Harrison dumped the lube and condoms onto the comforter so they would be in easy reach. "You want me to prep you or are you going to put on a show?"

As much as Harrison would love to watch a show, he hoped Owen would get himself ready so he didn't blow before he even pushed into that ass.

"No show. I'm too horny for that, but I will get myself ready. It'll go faster, and if you put your hands on me, I might blow before either of us is ready. It's been a while."

"For me too." Harrison took a condom from the pile and ripped it open.

He stroked his cock a couple times, but not too much because he didn't want to come yet. Like Owen, he was on the verge of exploding. He rolled the condom on while watching Owen reach for the slick and move to open himself up. Harrison held out a hand for some of the lube to make himself ready.

Owen might have said he wasn't going to put on a show, but he turned his ass to face Harrison and eased a finger inside his own hole. It was so fucking hot. Harrison had to squeeze his dick so he didn't burst. He closed his eyes when Owen used a second finger. He couldn't watch or there would be no sex. It didn't take long after that second finger for Owen to crawl toward him and straddle his thighs. No words were spoken as Owen took Harrison's dick and eased it inside his hole.

"Fuck."

"That's what we're aiming for here, Harrison." Owen smirked.

Harrison watched his new lover's face as the two of them became one. Once Owen was fully seated, he didn't move. The only sound was their harsh breathing as they stared at each other. Harrison needed another taste. He sat up, digging his heels into the mattress. He would need better leverage in a moment, but for now, he circled his arm around Owen's back and used the other to hold himself up. Owen's plump lips were begging to be kissed.

Owen leaned forward. The movement had Harrison's cock sliding outside cut that hot hole. He pulled Owen down and pushed himself up. They both groaned, and Harrison felt the vibration all the way to his toes. He couldn't get enough traction with Owen riding him. He took a quick kiss before switching their positions.

He hovered over Owen and stared down at the attractive man under him.

"Can't...need more...so good."

"Move. Now, Harrison." Owen closed his eyes and bit his lip.

No way could Harrison let Owen abuse his lip. He lapped at his lover's lips and sighed when he was let in. He moved his hips in a slow rhythm that didn't last long. Owen wrapped his legs around Harrison, trapping him, making his movements smaller and more intense. It was too much sensation and he was going to come, especially with Owen clinging to him. Every inch of skin touched in some way.

"So. Good. Tight. Owen." Harrison took one of Owen's legs and put it over his shoulder, getting a better angle to push deeper.

"Fast...er. Harrison. Soon. Oh, fuck, I'm gonna come." Owen's body was shaking under his.

"Wait for me. Close."

"Nggh."

Warm liquid covered his stomach. Some even got to his chest. Owen hadn't waited. Harrison pumped his hips a couple more times, his balls tightening. He was so close it was almost painful, he wanted it to go on and on, but his body was ready for the release. He threw his head back and groaned as he came in the condom. He collapsed on top of Owen and had to catch his breath before he rolled over.

Owen curled up next to him and placed his head on Harrison's chest. It felt like he'd come home, but it was way too soon for that. It had been too long and the happiness from his orgasm was going to his head—and not the little one.

"We should shower." Harrison was still out of breath, but managed to smooth his hand down Owen's back.

"Don't want to move." Owen snuggled in closer, rubbing his cheek against Harrison's chest.

"Me either. It was just a suggestion."

"Maybe later." Owen patted his chest then yawned.

"I…" Harrison yawned as well. "I can do later."

Harrison was drifting in and out of sleep. He wanted to bask in the fact that he'd finally met the man he'd been so obsessed with, but the emotions of the night were catching up to him — woman missing from his hotel and finally meeting Owen. He'd take the good with the bad.

He let himself drift off until he heard a soft snore coming from Owen. The good detective had to be exhausted after the night's events, not to mention the other kidnappings that had been happening. It made him happy that he'd gone into the private sector instead of joining the force. Sure, he had some stress, but nothing like what weighed Owen down.

Harrison shifted so he could wiggle out from under his new lover. He didn't want to disturb Owen's sleep. He could order some room service in a little bit so they could get something to eat. He didn't know about Owen, but he hadn't eaten since that morning and he was starving.

Shower first.

Cleaning up would take no time at all. Afterward, he could get food and see if Owen woke up. It was late, so he should probably forget the food and go back to sleep. One thing he learned a long time ago in the Army was that sleeping in any condition at the drop of a hat came in handy during combat situations.

After leaving the military, he promised himself he would indulge in what he wanted and right now Harrison craved pie. Being an adult had to have its perks, but he still needed to get cleaned up first.

One thing he loved about the rooms in the Totally Five Star was the bathrooms. The shower and toilet were in different sections. He walked into the smaller room with the vanity mirror, two sinks and the toilet. He shut the door behind him and continued on to the other room and shut that door too. Inside was a spa tub that was wonderful for soaking tired bones, but he didn't want to take time for that. The glass shower was separate from the tub and big enough for two. Unfortunately this time it would be just him. Maybe he could get Owen wet later. Just thinking about the sexy detective got him hard.

Harrison turned on the taps and stepped inside. The warm water felt good as it pounded against his body. He didn't plan on taking a long time. He just wanted to freshen up. Owen had used the Totally Five Star body wash and left it in the shower. Harrison picked it up, squeezed some on his hands and soaped up his body. He didn't think about the fact that Owen had used this soap on his own body not even an hour before. He had a hard enough time keeping his erection in check without sexy shower thoughts.

After rinsing, Harrison snatched up one of the fluffy towels to dry off. It was time to order pie. He walked out of the bathroom, drying off his hair. He'd have to find his clothes later, but for now, the towel would do.

Owen had rolled over in his sleep, the covers pushed to the end of the bed. Harrison should have covered him up before he'd gone to the shower. He moved to cover Owen up.

"Hmm... Harrison?"

"Hey." Harrison sat on the edge of the bed. He ran his fingers down Owen's back.

"Time to get up?"

"Not if you don't want to. I'm going to order something to eat. You want something?"

"Mmm."

"Go back to sleep." Harrison chuckled.

"Sorry." Owen sat up and rubbed his eyes.

"You've had a hard few weeks. Just relax for now. There will be time for work tomorrow."

"True, but I don't know if I can go back to sleep right this second." Owen scratched his stomach then wrinkled his nose. "I need a shower."

"How about I order us something while you clean up? Maybe we can take another one together later." Harrison winked.

Owen grinned and pushed at Harrison.

"Order me a grilled cheese."

Harrison watched Owen's ass as he walked into the bathroom. If he had been wearing pants, he would have had to adjust himself. As it was, he left the towel on the bed and went to the phone. He put in an order for two gourmet grilled cheese sandwiches with Monterey jack cheese, some fries, drinks and a couple pieces of chocolate truffle pie with cherries and whipped cream on top. After making sure it was charged to him and not the room, he hung up and waited for Owen to join him.

He should get up and grab his pants, but he was being lazy. Harrison didn't have much downtime. He must have drifted off, because the next thing he knew, there was a knock at the door. He was startled by the sound and jumped up over the chair to get to cover so the shrapnel couldn't hit him.

It took him a few minutes to realize where he was. Harrison's face heated and he looked to see if Owen had seen his reaction. When the dreams of Ethan came, they hit him hard and it took a bit for Harrison to focus on where he really was. By the time he'd snapped out of it, Owen had the food set up on the small table in the room.

"You okay?" Owen stopped what he was doing to look at him.

"I'm good."

Owen gave him a nod. He sat at the table. Harrison joined him. He was happy Owen didn't push. Usually if someone saw him freak out, they were all over him to explain or to try to make him feel better.

"Mmm. I needed this."

"I wanted pie, but after you said something about grilled cheese, I had to have one too."

"There is just something about the cheesy goodness that makes me feel at home."

Harrison took a bite and had to agree. The sandwich made him think about his childhood. Days when Ethan was still with him. God, he missed him. Now wasn't the time to think about old memories. It took a while for him to shake off the melancholy that followed one of his nightmares.

"I know we just met, but if you want to talk, I'll listen. No pressure." Owen placed a hand on Harrison's arm.

Harrison had drifted off again.

"Thanks. I'm fine, really." Harrison smiled at Owen. "Maybe after a couple dates."

Owen smiled back. Harrison took that as a great sign. He did want to see the detective again. He wasn't sure if he'd share Ethan with Owen, but it was nice that the option was there.

"I do seem to recall someone saying we might need another shower."

Harrison had to laugh. "I did. Dessert first."

"You got it. That pie looks delicious. What is it?"

"It is a very good cherry truffle. The Totally Five Star has the best on the strip. The chef might think I have a sweet tooth."

"That is good to know."

"Yeah, it's also nice that we have a gym."

They both laughed. Harrison's dream was starting to fade. And he was grateful to Owen for just being there for him.

Chapter Nine

Raymond turned on the news. He was hoping the police had found the first body because he was ready to take the next girl out. He wanted to perfect his system. He didn't *need* to kill another yet, but the latest woman he'd taken was pushing him. If she was afraid, she wasn't showing it. The fear in the eyes of his victims was why the whole adventure was fun. This one was just pissing him off. Plus, she'd come from the Totally Five Star, and offing her would be all the sweeter for it. He should murder her now while he was on the high from grabbing her right out from under that cop's nose. It would also help show the police force looking like a joke. It would also help his pattern of having no real pattern into becoming an actual thing.

There was still no report of the corpse in the desert. By now it had to have been picked apart. His clue might be gone. If he wasn't careful, the first body wouldn't be connected with him. That wouldn't do. Raymond was going to have to make the women easier to find. He was ticked because they should have found her already. The attention he deserved wasn't happening. He slammed his hand on the table. Things weren't going by his timeline.

"That's it. Another one is going to die."

Tonight he would kill his latest victim, then he would go back out and take another woman, maybe two. This time he'd do a little searching. His first woman had been a local. He should get another one of those. He'd taken too many out-of-towners. They might not be missed as soon as a local would be.

What he needed to figure out was how to scare Vegas. If the cops wouldn't tell the city, maybe he could. There had to be a way. He really hated to do an anonymous call. He could get a burner phone, but he didn't want any trace of him associated with the case and he had a big fear of leaving a loose end. What if they recorded him, which they probably would? They could do some sort of voice recognition, then where would he be? In jail on death row and he wasn't going out that way.

He could see the disappointment on his grandparents' faces if he were arrested. It made him want to stab or shoot them, but he'd have to be patient. He wanted their money and there was no way even a hint of foul play would hover over their deaths. That money was rightfully his and he wouldn't ruin it. He'd take out his anger on the women. Channeling it that way would help ease some of his rage. He needed that outlet right now. He was supposed to have family dinner with them soon.

Raymond stood and walked away from his cold breakfast on the table. He wasn't hungry anymore. He clicked the television off. It was time to go visit his girls. Give them the good news that there were going to be at least two more joining them soon and one of them would be leaving. Their tears would get him through his day. After work, he'd kill one, let them stew all day wondering who it would be. The physiological part of this was one aspect he didn't think about, but he was really enjoying it.

Raymond contemplated dumping the next body right on the stairs of the police station, but he knew such a bold move would get him caught before he could finish his plans.

He wanted his fifteen minutes of fame, but he would get that anonymously. Raymond didn't need his name attached. At least not yet. When he was safely in Dubai, he would contact them and confess. Then he'd laugh at pulling one over on everyone.

All his efforts would be worth it. Raymond whistled as he threw out his breakfast and washed the dishes. He had to get ready for his shift at the hotel. He'd have to be quick about it if he wanted to visit his hidey hole. No way he'd miss that high.

The phone rang. He just knew that meant his day was going in the shitter.

"Hello?"

"Hello, dear. Just checking in. Your pappy and I will be in Vegas tonight. Dinner?"

"Tonight?" Leave it to his grandmother to ruin his plans.

It seemed that it always happened. Fucking family.

"Yes. I told you last week we'd be there today."

"Sorry. You are correct. I will meet you wherever you and grandfather would like to go."

"We'll just meet you at the Totally Five Star."

"I work today." Raymond kept the frustration out of his voice. He was a good actor.

"When do you get off? We'll just meet you after your shift."

Raymond wasn't even going to argue with her. It wasn't worth it. He'd have to put off his plans until later tonight or tomorrow. Hopefully it would give the cops time to find his first body. Maybe he should thank his grandmother for keeping him on track. He wouldn't, but it was a nice thought. He didn't have many of those.

"That sounds like a good plan."

"I'll let Pappy know. He'll be so happy to see you."

He had no idea what world his grandmother lived in, but his grandfather would be happy to *never* see him again. It was like the man could see through him.

"I can't wait to see you both. Tonight around five?"

"Wonderful. See you then, sweetie."

Raymond hung up the phone. The frustration was building. He couldn't go see his women before work because he would kill one right then and there. He couldn't afford that. It was sloppy and sloppy got caught.

Chapter Ten

Owen was going to be late for work. He should be relaxed after all of the sex he had last night, but when he'd woken up, all he could think about was the missing woman who'd been taken right out from under his nose. The tension from the past week came back.

He shouldn't blame himself. It wasn't like he'd been on duty. And truth be told, she might have been taken even if he hadn't been there. It was a little egotistical of him to think she was taken because of him, but the guilt was high with this case. He had a feeling of doom hanging over him. Like something bad was going to happen and soon. They didn't have any ransom calls and they hadn't found any bodies. It probably had to do with the little boy he'd met when he was first given the case. Owen wanted to give him his mother back, but as the days and weeks passed, he was afraid that wasn't going to happen. It made him think of his sister and niece. He didn't know what he'd do if something happened to either of them.

The fucker doing this was going to explode soon, and Owen had to hope that it wouldn't come with the death of the woman he'd taken. He didn't want to have to go back to that little boy and tell him his mommy was dead.

There was no whistling today, even though he had great reason to and usually would have after a night of hot sex. He drove home in a fog of second guessing every move he'd made on the case. He'd said his goodbyes to Harrison. Owen would see him again, if not on a personal level then on a professional one. It was odd that the Totally Five Star had been hit twice. None of the other places the victims had been taken from had more than one woman associated with them, plus there were plenty of resorts in Vegas to pick from. Owen had gone over this before. He was reaching and knew it, but it was still circling his brain.

Maybe he'd have Polubinsky check it out. Get a new set of eyes on that hotel. He might be a bit biased. His partner could take a look at Harrison to get him checked off the suspect list. Not that they had a big list. Shit. He probably shouldn't have slept with Harrison before clearing him, but he really didn't think Harrison had anything to do with the kidnappings. The man had been there when that group of women had come up to them about their missing friend. Harrison would have to be a pretty great actor to pull off his reaction. Owen would still have Polubinsky check things out so all of their T's were crossed and I's were dotted.

It didn't take him long to get ready now that his mom was out of the house. His sister must have still been in bed. Gabbi was probably at the bus stop or already on her way to school. He'd taken a shower at the hotel, which was what was making him late. Harrison liked him wet. It would be worth hearing his partner complain so he could tell him he'd gotten laid. Owen smiled. He loved fucking with Jeff just as much as Jeff liked messing with him.

Once he got to the station, he rushed up the steps and headed to his desk. He didn't even have time to sit before his partner was shouting at him.

"What the fuck, Carpenter!" Jeff stood and pointed at Owen.

"I don't know, Polubinsky? What the fuck?" Owen pointed back.

"I get a call saying another chick has been kidnapped and you're off on some holiday or something." Jeff had stopped pointing and had his hands on his hips.

That was his serious face too, and Owen had to stop himself from grinning. Jeff tried to look so tough, but he wasn't as badass as he thought he was.

"Shut your face. I was supposed to have some downtime and you know it. I cut into off time to investigate while it was fresh. We got diddly squat." Owen sat at his desk.

"Shit. I know man, it's just—" Jeff put his hands on his desk and bowed his head.

"It is all around a fucked-up situation and we both feel overwhelmed. I'm sure the captain will start a task force. Hopefully today. We need to find them before…" Owen's boss strode across the precinct toward him and his partner. That couldn't be good.

"Before…what?" Jeff looked back over at him.

"Maybe he was going to say before we got a body? Too late." Their captain threw a file on Owen's desk.

"No." Owen didn't want to open it. He was afraid it would be Jade Chase. That name was forever etched in his brain and it would never go away if she were killed.

"Yes. They found her late last night. Forensics has already been on scene. They're backed up, so I don't know when we'll get cause of death from the autopsy.

Field agents speculate that she was suffocated because there weren't any contusions anywhere on the body. You two need to head out to the dump site and take a look to see if you can find anything."

"Do you have an ID?" Owen stopped looking at the folder long enough to glance up at his boss.

"Jade Chase was on the driver's license on the body, but the photo didn't match."

"Jade Chase?" Owen flipped through his notes, his heart racing. "Shit. This isn't good. I met her son when I did an interview with her boyfriend. Fuck."

His worst fears were coming to life. The clock just switched to lightning fast. It was ticking down and Jade was on the other end. Probably the latest one too, Molli.

"Yes. We still don't have an ID on the victim, but we know the two women were together. It's a clue. Hopefully this fucker screwed up. Get out there and see if he left anything behind. We have uni's canvassing the scene, looking for witnesses. You two go get a feel. Later this afternoon we'll be doing a press conference. Get me what you can. You two will lead up the task force. Take whoever you need. This guy needs to be stopped before we find any more damn bodies."

"Yes, sir," Owen and Jeff said in unison.

Their captain walked away, probably going to his office. The boss hated doing press conferences and had to prepare himself. Owen didn't blame him, he wouldn't want to do them either.

Owen was going to have to go back to Tommy and tell him about his mother. He hated it when kids were connected in any way to a case. An event like this could tear a child apart and he shouldn't have to deal with death of a parent at such a young age.

"You need to stop thinking about that kid and get your head in the game. We'll find his mom." Jeff stood up again and gathered his gun and badge out of his desk drawer.

"Dead or alive?" Owen got up as well. He hadn't had time to put his badge and gun away so he was ready to go.

"Alive." Jeff gave a hard nod. He was trying to convince himself, Owen could tell.

"I have to believe that." Owen hoped luck was on their side and the fucker had messed up.

"So do I. Let's get out to the scene. What more can you tell me about the latest kidnapping?" Jeff headed out to the front of the precinct.

Owen followed, trying to keep up with Jeff's long strides.

"She fits his type. Shit." Owen stopped walking.

"What?" Jeff turned to look at him.

"So does my sister. We need to swing by my place before going to the crime scene." Owen moved again, this time making Jeff keep up with *him*. His sister was not going on their list of victims.

"What are the odds?"

"I don't know, but I want her to be aware of what is going on so she'll pay attention, maybe have her stay away from the hotels."

"Your sister? We're talking about Susan."

"I only have one sister, shithead."

"I know, but she isn't so…ahh…well, you know." Jeff shrugged.

"Yes, I know, but she's getting better. They're moving in with me for a while. With Mom in a home now, I have more than enough room." They'd reached their department vehicle. Jeff had the keys so he moved for the passenger door.

"And you can keep an eye on her." Jeff smirked.

That was the problem with being friends with his partner. Jeff knew too much about Owen's life and had spent hours listening to Owen bitch about his sister and her life choices.

"That too. I love my sister. I do. But she isn't one with much common sense."

"That's what Gabbi is for."

Owen smiled. He loved his niece so much and vowed she wouldn't grow up too fast. Not under his watch. It was time for her to be a kid again.

"God, I love that girl like she's my own. This way Gabbi can be more of a kid and stop worrying about her mother."

"All right, then. We need to talk to her so you can get back to the case and we can catch this bastard."

Jeff started the car and they were off to his house. Hopefully Susan would be awake. It didn't really matter because he'd be waking her up for this. It was important. The odds were nothing would happen, but Owen didn't want to take that chance with his family. Tonight he'd talk with Gabbi too. She didn't fit the profile, but she needed to be more cautious too.

When it came to serial kidnappers or killers they could evolve the longer they kept taking and killing.

Neither of them spoke. They let the radio take control of the silence. They both had too much on their minds with the case taking a turn to murder. It was escalating and it needed to be stopped before the bodies began piling up. The press conference would help keep the women in Vegas alert—at least the locals. They had to hope the vacationing women caught the news. It was a big clusterfuck and would probably put the people of Vegas in a panic, which is why they'd held off as long as they had. Now with the murdered woman, they had no choice but to let the public know.

Owen hated that they'd give this fuck any amount of air time. He'd probably get off on it. Owen had to pray it wouldn't cause the kidnapper to murder another woman. And why was he switching up the driver's licenses? It was an odd signature. Owen would have to do some research and see if it had been used before. It might narrow it down if they had more information.

He opened the file and glanced at the pictures of the dead woman. It could be his sister's picture or Jade's in that folder. The woman appeared to be sleeping. She was fully clothed, if a little dirty. It didn't seem like she'd been sexually assaulted. The autopsy would confirm that. It was a small relief. Very small.

There weren't a whole lot of notes. The body was found in an isolated part of the desert away from the Vegas lights. They were lucky they'd found her when they did. Not too many scavengers had gotten to her. She'd been laid out like she was sleeping and it looked like she was holding Jade's driver's license. No footprints were evident in the dirt. They might have been swept away. The perp was careful. But he'd mess up. They always did. And when that happened, Owen would be there to take the bastard down.

Chapter Eleven

Harrison had gone back to his apartment after Owen left. He wanted to get ready for the day, but he also wanted to call his buddy from home and get him to add that extra camera. He felt bad because he trusted all of his employees. Hell, he'd vetted them all. The dealers and security personnel were more closely researched than the kitchen or housekeeping staff, but it was his job to oversee them all before they were hired.

The Totally Five Star had a reputation to uphold, and it was his job to make sure people were safe and had a good time. He shouldn't take it personally, but he was. It was his hotel, damn it. James Conroy the III, the CEO of the Totally Five Star chain, had hired Harrison personally. He'd had a few meetings with Mr. Conroy's personal assistant Claudia Bauer. She was a tough cookie and hadn't let him see Mr. Conroy until he'd been through background checks and a multitude of questions. No way was he going to let Mr. Conroy down. The man had given him a chance after Harrison had left the military and Harrison would always remember that.

Only way to make sure no one else was taken from the vicinity of the hotel was to add more cameras and to fix the dead spot. If it was someone in his hotel kidnapping women, Harrison would make sure they were caught. If anyone else was taken, he would add outside patrols to the roster. First he wanted to make sure none of his employees could be behind it. It wouldn't do to put the kidnapper on patrol. When he got into work, he'd do some more background checks. See if he'd missed anything. Harrison would start with the security people.

Harrison had time to get ready, but maybe he would go in early. He was working the swing shift today. He liked to mix it up. It was hell on his sleep schedule, but it kept his employees on their toes. A person couldn't get complacent in his position and neither could his employees. He treated them like a well-trained military unit. Which was another reason he didn't want it to be a member of his staff. But he couldn't know everything about everybody. Today he would certainly try.

He rummaged through his closet. It was time for him to get some suits dry cleaned. He was running out of things to wear. Harrison finally found something that would be presentable. He laid it over the chair and went to the kitchen in just his T-shirt and boxer briefs. He didn't want to get anything on his suit. He opened the fridge door only to find a leftover pizza, beer and a jar of pickles. Obviously he needed to go to the store as well. Harrison had no idea how long that pizza had been there. He grabbed the jar of pickles. They were still good, according to the sell-by date. It was better than nothing, but he needed to remember to brush his teeth after eating them because he didn't want to offend his staff with his pickle breath.

They had just been visited by Armand Cassells. He was a world-renowned chef and one of the chain's directors. He'd done an overhaul on the kitchen and the food was better than ever. Which was why Harrison had an empty fridge and needed more trips to the gym.

He'd go into work earlier and order something to his office. Most wouldn't think anything of it. He really did live and breathe the Totally Five Star. So much so that he wondered if he had time for a relationship. He wanted to see where things went with Owen. The man intrigued him. Harrison got hard thinking about the good detective. There was so much they could explore. It seemed they had the same values. Owen had stepped up to the plate when that group of women had rushed them last night. He'd put off his personal time to do a perimeter search. He was someone Harrison could grow to really like.

Would Owen be willing to cut back on his hours to go on dates? Is that something Owen would even want? They'd only know each other a few hours. Last night could have been only a one-night stand for Owen, which would be fine, if disappointing. Harrison was just going to have to take it a day at a time. He hadn't even gotten Owen's number, but he knew who would have it—Drew. He'd have to see if the dealer was working today. He didn't have their schedules. That was up to the pit boss.

Thinking about last night had his cock at attention. Fuck. Now he was going to have to take care of that too, hunger be damned. Harrison squeezed his cock through his boxers. It was time to take this to the bathroom—two birds, one stone. He started the shower, his dick not going down at all because images of Owen were filtering through his head as he remembered the awe on his new lover's face when he came.

When the water was just right, he stepped in and grabbed the soap. Harrison tugged on his erection, slow strokes to start with. He had to put a hand on the shower wall to steady himself, his head down, water pouring over it. Picturing Owen rocking on his dick made him speed up. It was going to be quick and dirty. He stood on tiptoes, thrusting into his hand.

"Owen!" Harrison collapsed against the wall, his seed flowing down the drain, the tiles cold against his skin. The water was still warm, but barely. He had to add more hot water to make it comfortable enough to finish washing up.

His stomach grumbled. Harrison rushed into getting on a fresh pair of boxers and a white undershirt before going back to the kitchen to the jar of pickles on the counter. It still wasn't the best brunch, but it would do until he got to work. Right now he had to think about doing his job and if that included catching a kidnapper, so be it. He crunched into the last of the pickles then washed his hands. It was going to be a long day.

* * * *

Harrison settled behind his desk. He'd already called down to the kitchen to get something for lunch, the pickles long since wearing off. Now he could focus on looking deeper into his employees' lives. As much as he hated it, he had to do it for his own peace of mind. He glanced at his watch. He still had a few hours until he'd be officially on the clock. If he found out anything that would be useful, he'd see if he could find Drew and get Owen's number. If not, he'd call the police station.

He started with the files he already had. Nothing jumped out at him. It was frustrating. A knock at his door was a great relief.

Rachel, one of his best tech people, poked her head into his office. "Boss, there are a couple detectives out here who would like to see you, and the kitchen said lunch was a bit behind, it'd be up in a few minutes."

"Send them in, thanks."

"Sure thing." Rachel left without much fanfare.

It was one of the reasons he liked her. After she left, two men walked in. One he recognized—Owen. The other guy must be his partner.

"Harrison. Hello." Owen moved closer and held out his hand.

Harrison lifted an eyebrow and smiled. He took the offered hand and shook it. Owen blushed. It was cute.

"Owen."

"This is my partner, Jeff Polubinsky."

"Detective Polubinsky." Harrison held out his hand.

"Jeff is fine." The detective wiggled his eyebrows and smiled.

Harrison wondered what that was all about, but Owen started talking.

"I filled Jeff in on what happened last night—"

"I see."

"No! Not that. Well, some of that. Not... Oh, fuck, shut me up."

"What my partner is trying to say is he filled me in on the missing woman." Jeff's look encompassed the office. "Is this room secure?"

"It will be if I close us in. Hold on." Harrison moved around the two men and shut the door.

A bumbling Owen was even cuter than a blushing one. It was another side to the detective and Harrison really liked it. Well, he'd seen some of it when they'd first met, but he'd thought it was a fluke, first meeting kind of thing. Now that he knew it was a part of Owen's character, he found he liked it even more.

"They found a body. We just came back from the dump site."

"Molli?"

"No. Still nothing on her. We haven't identified her yet. But the perp is escalating. Jeff is going to interview some of your staff if that's okay."

"Sure. I was just going over their employment records before you got here. We could have lunch brought up for us and go over them. See how you want to approach the interviews."

"That would be great. Are you sure you're okay with that?"

"Yes, and if you want, you can interview me first so we can get that out of the way. I want to do what I can to help you guys catch whoever is taking these women. The Totally Five Star has a reputation to keep up and I don't want people to think we are holding back when it comes to the police. You'll have my full cooperation."

"Sounds great." Owen sat in one of the chairs in front of Harrison's desk.

Harrison left the door to go to his desk. "I already called down for my lunch, what can I get you two?"

"I think I'll have another grilled cheese. The one last night was amazing. I wish I could make it as well." Owen smiled at him.

"We have a new kitchen staff, so they've changed things up."

"The food was great before, so I can only imagine."

"You should try the Italian." Harrison should stop talking. He was just ordering a meal for them, not going on another date. This was business. They had to find out who was behind terrorizing Vegas by taking women off the street.

"I'll have to. Next time." Owen seemed like he wanted to say something else, but he glanced over at his partner and didn't say anything.

"I'll have a burger and fries." Jeff didn't seem phased by the conversation.

Of course they were talking food, not sex, but Harrison was super sensitive to the vibe going on between him and Owen. Owen wore his suit well, and Harrison had a thing for men in suits. If he didn't want to embarrass himself, he was going to have to stop thinking about Owen naked in the shower with the water running over his hard body.

"What do you want on the burger?" Back to the food. He could handle that.

"Just some tomato."

Harrison placed the call and told them not to bring his up until the others were done. With the call finished, he looked at the two detectives in front of him.

"It shouldn't take too long. These documents haven't really helped me with much. I did a deep security search before hiring each person. Many of them have military backgrounds, but maybe a fresh pair of eyes can see something I haven't." Harrison gave Owen and Jeff a couple folders.

"The person we're searching for probably isn't even in here. There might not be any rhyme or reason to the fact that two of the victims came from this hotel." Owen was trying to reassure him.

Harrison knew that it was a slim chance the kidnapper and now killer came from the Totally Five Star, he just wanted to make sure. He had to for his own peace of mind. If the detectives cleared everyone, it would make him feel better.

"I know. I talked to the manager to let him know what was going on with the new camera. He agreed to let my guy come in late tonight to put a couple cameras in the dead spot, like you suggested. I didn't put a work order in for them, but one of the heads of the chain, Mr. Sosa, was called so the main office is aware of the situation. I have a friend doing it so it's off the books, and for right now, they're okay with it, but I'm sure they will be sending someone in to help if we need them to. After we go through all of the records and are sure it isn't someone from my security team, I will have them start to patrol the outside of the hotel as well."

"That sounds like a good idea. Will you set up the monitor for the dead spot in here?" Jeff peered up from the file he was reading.

"Yes. Even if you clear everyone, I think it is best. I want to keep an eye on it. I can't believe we didn't get it fixed a long time ago. I never noticed it until last night." Harrison picked up another document.

"No one was prepared for this kind of thing to happen. I mean, sure, we get the occasional murder, rape or mugging, but nothing this big since 2005 when those escorts were killed and their bodies found in Illinois. And that one guy back in 1988 who killed his ex-wife. There could have been others, but mostly we deal with everyday violence that sucks. I personally have never been on a case like this." Owen reached out and put his hand on Harrison's.

He did feel better and hoped the person behind the kidnappings didn't work with him.

"Me either. You can't beat yourself up about this. This guy isn't getting away." Jeff shuffled through a few more files.

"Okay. I only have a handful of papers left. I have an updated search going on my computer." There was a knock on the door. "And that is lunch."

Harrison was ready for an afternoon of police work, then his life could go back to routine. He was ready for that and maybe a couple dates with the handsome detective.

Chapter Twelve

Raymond kept glancing behind him. His boss had been holed up in the office for a long time with those two detectives. The one he'd followed was in there. The one with the pretty sister who fit his *type*.

"Hey, Rachel, what's going on?" Raymond tilted his head toward Mr. Boone's door.

"I don't know. He didn't say anything before he closed himself up with those two officers."

"It's been a few hours." He looked back over, willing the door to open. He wanted to know if they were talking about him.

There was no way they could know it was him behind anything. He'd been careful. So he should stop worrying before he did give something away. If it had only been the blond guy, he wouldn't be so curious. He'd been there before. It was the other detective coming with him that was worth worrying over.

"Yep." Rachel shrugged.

She wasn't going to be any help. Usually she was a fount of information. She had the boss's ear. At least more so than he did. He was just a lowly worker who watched the monitor for card counters. Fun times. He didn't have the training of some of the others. A lot of his coworkers were ex-military. He was the grandson of a friend who had needed a job. It didn't take much to watch monitors all day.

He was still pissed that he hadn't had time to go see the women this morning. And it was going to be late before he got back there since he was having dinner with his grandparents, who sucked the fun out of everything.

Raymond peered at the clock. He still had a few hours of work left before the dinner. He hoped he could keep his temper in check. For once, he hoped they would acknowledge that he was doing what they wanted him to do. Maybe they'd release his trust fund. Would that make him stop his course of action? No. He was in this for the notoriety now. He could kill the woman he had and stop there, but that would just make him a dud. He wanted a body count. A high one that would put him up there with the big names like Ted Bundy or John Wayne Gacy. Their numbers weren't as high as Gary Ridgway, but that name wasn't as well known. Not like the other two. Raymond wanted to strike fear in people. It was quickly becoming an obsession. At first, he'd gone into the kidnapping-murder thing because he was bored and he couldn't kill his grandparents if he wanted the money. Detectives always suspected the family first, and he hadn't figured out a way to get rid of his grandparents yet without implicating himself. It had to look natural and not implicate him. His grandparents' friends would point their fingers at him if anything even remotely looked fishy. Raymond's grandfather talked trash about him whenever he could. If Raymond had to hear one more time how lazy he was, he would explode. It was his grandfather's fault he had a job in the first place.

Tonight he was going to kill his second woman. He'd still suffocate her like the other one, but he would do it differently this time. He wanted to watch the life leave her body. The first one he'd drugged and she hadn't even struggled when he'd put the pillow over her face. This one he would take his time with. He'd drug her then tie her to the table, wait for her to wake up, then he'd use his hands around her neck. He would look death in the face. He was ready.

The first kill hadn't satisfied him as much as he'd thought it would. Maybe he was escalating faster than he'd planned, but he didn't care. This was about him now. He could make a new plan. There were no rules.

He went back to his appointed screen. Nothing was going on this afternoon. It got busier at night, but he was out of there at four-thirty before the real action started. He rested his chin on his fist and thought about what was going to happen later tonight.

Lost in his daydream, he almost didn't hear the office door open.

"I'll see you out." Mr. Boone walked out with the other two close on his heels.

"Thanks, Harrison, but you don't have to." The blond turned to look at the other guy. "Why don't you head on out and I'll meet you out front?"

The other detective shook his head and left without saying a word.

"I don't mind, Owen." Mr. Boone leaned against the door frame.

"I know." Owen glanced around then leaned closer.

It was harder for Raymond to hear what was being said, but he managed. It looked like the detective was asking his boss out. Dinner at his place. And his sister wouldn't be there. The sister who looked like the other women he had caged in his warehouse. She was going to be at the movies. A late showing. She'd leave after dinner. He would just have to be outside Owen's house before she left. He could follow her.

Taking a family member would make the police do more than sit on their asses and keep the information out of the news. Raymond would have to be extra careful and up his kidnapping to get his count high enough. Yes. He could do this. All he had to do was get through dinner with his grandparents. That shouldn't take too long. They were old and needed their sleep. Raymond was going to take that detective's sister. And he was going to kill her. Eventually. He'd let her suffer in the cage for a while. He would make it so Owen found the body. He smiled and went back to watching the monitor. All the scenarios running through his head were enough to make him hard. He was starting to enjoy his extracurricular activities more than he ever thought he would.

Chapter Thirteen

Owen stirred the sauce in the pot. Spaghetti was easy and something he could make. He was an okay cook. Nothing like the food at the Totally Five Star, but it would do in a pinch. Maybe he should have made lasagna, but it was too late now. He already had the noodles boiling.

"Are you sure you don't want me to leave earlier? Gabbi is already at her friend's. I can go out to dinner." Susan poked a fork into a meatball.

"Stay out of that. You can have some with dinner. There is no need to go out. I have plenty." Owen put the spoon on a plate he had resting on the stove.

"You really like this guy, don't you?" Susan left the fork in the meatball, but moved away from the counter.

"I could." Owen shrugged. He'd have to learn more about Harrison, but they seemed to fit and the sexual chemistry was off the charts. Owen wanted to explore more of that — a lot more.

"I'm happy for you."

"Thanks." He turned to look at his sister.

He wondered if she was happy. He hoped she was, or that she was getting there. He loved his sister and wanted her there with him.

"I saw Mom yesterday."

"How did that go?" Owen moved closer to Susan.

It was hard watching their mom forget them. It had been easier with their dad. He'd died quickly. It didn't mean it still didn't hurt, but it was better than this long, drawn-out disease with no cure.

"Better than I thought it would. I took Gabbi with me. She knew who we were, for a while. A couple times she thought Gabbi was me."

"She calls me by Dad's name sometimes."

"I hate it." Susan crossed her arms over her chest, closing herself off from him.

No way was he going to let Susan shut herself down. That was how she got into trouble. Thinking no one was there for her, but he was and he needed her to know that.

"Me too. I know soon she won't remember us at all, but it'll be okay. We'll be there for her." He walked over to Susan and hugged her tightly for a second before moving back to the stove.

"We will. And I thought about it."

"Thought about what?"

"Moving in here."

"You gonna?" Owen took a spoon and dipped it into the sauce then took a taste.

More salt. He picked up the shaker and added a bit and put some onions and garlic in the pot as well. It was almost time to add the meatballs.

"Yes. I shouldn't because you need your space. I mean, you had Mom living here with you for a long time and she just moved out, but I need to start thinking about Gabbi. Here she can be a kid and stop worrying about me. We can put down roots. It will be good for both of us."

"This house is big enough for all of us. I don't need to be alone. I work long hours as it is and —"

"That's just it. When you're off, you need your downtime, not the two of us in the way, but I'm going to be my usual selfish self and take you up on your offer."

"I wouldn't have offered if I didn't mean it." Owen took the meatballs and added them to his sauce then turned down the heat to let it simmer.

"Yes, you would have."

"Okay, yes, I would have, but I do mean it. I love you both. I *want* you here." Owen turned the noodles off, strained them and cooled them with water so they stopped cooking before he would finish them off in the sauce later. He set them aside so he could focus on his sister while the sauce simmered.

"What about the new guy?"

Owen put the potholders down on the counter and faced his sister again. "If he can't understand my need to help my family, than he isn't the guy I thought he was and not worth my time."

"At least *you* have your priorities straight."

"Come on, Susan, don't be so hard on yourself."

"Someone needs to. You and Mom have been too easy on me. I know. It's time I started acting like an adult."

"You've got this, sis. I know you do, and you should know that I will always be here for you."

"I know you are and I love you for it. I screw up. A lot. You think I don't know, but I do. No." Susan held up her hand. "I'm better now. I am. It's been a struggle and I'll always be an alcoholic, but I know with you in my corner, I can fight this thing. Now go get cleaned up before I cry. I'll watch this stuff until you're done."

Owen was proud of his sister. It had to be hard for her to move in with him. He was sure it felt like she was going backward with her life, but he knew it was the right thing for both of them. He pulled her into a hug and took a few minutes before he let her go.

He was happy she was staying for dinner. If he wanted to get serious with Harrison, he'd have to meet his family sooner or later and it might as well be now. Owen's life could be hectic with work, so he took the time as he had it. And right now, he really didn't have a whole lot of time with a crazy person terrorizing his city.

Sometimes he wished he had a nine-to-five job, but when he caught a perpetrator and the victim had closure, it was the best feeling in the world. He liked helping people and putting the bad guys behind bars. He could have gone to some small town, but Vegas was his home.

Owen got under the water and remembered his shower with Harrison. He wanted to do that again. Soon, if possible. He hurried up because he still needed to add the noodles to the sauce and put the garlic bread in the oven. He also wanted to get a salad together. When he had a chance to cook, he enjoyed it. It was something that calmed his nerves. Not as well as a night at the Totally Five Star, but it would do in a pinch.

He toweled off and tugged on his jeans and a nice shirt. It wasn't a date, but it was dinner at his house, so he wasn't going to get too dressed up.

When he got back to the kitchen, his sister was messing with the sauce.

"Hey, I can finish up." He bumped hips with her and smiled.

"Okay. After dinner I'll meet up with my friends for the movie and give you some...alone time." Susan wiggled her eyebrows at him.

Owen laughed. He liked that his sister was in a playful mood. This is how he remembered her the best. Growing up, his little sister could always make him laugh. He didn't know when it had turned around for her, but he was happy she was making her way back. It really was a good thing she was moving in.

"Sounds like a plan." Owen looked down at his watch. "Harrison should be here any minute. I'm going to put the garlic bread in. Could you add the noodles to the sauce?"

"Sure thing."

They worked in harmony until the doorbell rang. Owen turned the oven off so the bread wouldn't burn but would still be hot when they ate then went to let Harrison in.

He jogged to the door and opened it to see Harrison in a tight pair of jeans and an even tighter shirt. His arms looked like they could bust out of the sleeves. Owen wanted to watch the show. He licked his lips and looked up into Harrison's blue eyes. He had the urge to climb up on him and suck on his lips. He cleared his throat and got a hold of himself. They were going to eat. Dinner first. Owen's sister was there for fuck's sake.

"Hello, Harrison."

"Owen. I brought some beer. I wasn't sure what we were having for dinner, but beer is good with anything." Harrison handed him the six-pack.

"Thanks. Follow me. I'll put this in the fridge."

If Owen had a bit more wiggle in his step, so what? He liked the fact that Harrison was probably staring at his ass.

"Harrison Boone, this is Susan Carpenter. Susan, Harrison." He put the beer in the fridge.

Susan shook Harrison's hand.

"Nice to meet you."

"Same here, Susan."

"Dinner is ready. Susan, you want to bring the bread? I'll get the pasta. We'll put it on the table and serve from there."

"Got it." Susan went to the stove.

"What can I do?"

"If you want to grab the pitcher of lemonade, a beer for me and whatever you want then meet us at the table, that'd be great." Owen motioned to the door that led to the dining room.

Owen wiped his damp hands down his pants. He shouldn't be nervous, but he was. He'd invited a man he hardly knew into his home. A man he'd already had sex with and liked.

Once they were settled at the table, Owen felt a bit better. At least more comfortable.

"Everything smells wonderful. It's been a while since I've had a home-cooked meal. Usually I order from the hotel. I won't even tell you how my fridge looked when I went home this morning." Harrison shook his head.

"I usually do takeout, but I like to cook."

"He's good at it. Gabbi loves this breakfast bake thing he does."

"Gabbi isn't here?" Harrison looked around like he expected to see her.

"No. She's spending the night at a friend's. I'll be out of your hair after dinner. Going to a late movie, probably go out for coffee later. In other words, I'll be out for a while, just so you know." Susan winked at him.

Owen didn't even bother to respond. She was trying to embarrass him and she would, if he let her.

Harrison cleared his throat. "That's...uh...good to know."

"Ignore her. She thinks she'll embarrass me, but she won't."

"I could tell Harrison about—"

"Again...she *won't* embarrass me." Owen glared at his sister.

"You're right. I won't." Susan laughed.

Harrison glanced back and forth between them. Owen wondered what he was thinking.

"I caught a bit of the press conference. You looked nice standing there, but I wish it wasn't for something so awful." Harrison ate a bit of the spaghetti and it took a moment for Owen to realize he'd said something.

He needed to stop thinking about sex. At least until later. He took a big gulp of his beer before saying something.

"Yeah, but the public needed to know. I already warned Susan earlier today. She fits his profile, which is one of the reasons she is going with friends. They're picking her up here in a little bit."

"I hope you catch the bastard soon. This sucks. I'll probably stick close to home until you do catch him. Well, not tonight." Susan grinned at him.

"So, what is it you do, Susan?"

"I'm in between jobs right now. Bit of a rough patch, but I'm getting back on my feet thanks to Owen. He's a good guy." Susan shot Harrison a hard look, like she was trying to say something to him with her eyes.

"Yes, he is." Harrison winked at him. "It's good he has a protective sister too. So, what kind of work will you be looking for?"

"I'm an administrative assistant. So I do a lot of paperwork." Susan shrugged. "Hopefully I can find something, but if not, I make a good waitress." Susan went back to eating.

"She'll find something." Owen reached over and squeezed his sister's hand.

"What about you? Any family?" Owen crunched into his garlic bread and waited for Harrison's answer.

Chapter Fourteen

Harrison thought about the question for a second. He didn't have any blood family, but he had plenty of family from his time in the military.

"My dad is dead, and I don't have any siblings. It's been me and my mom for a long time. I try to bring her out to Vegas when I can. We were close, growing up. My unit from the military is all the family I really need — well, and my mom. The guys and I get together every couple of months."

"That's good. Our dad isn't with us anymore and our mom is in a home because her Alzheimer's is getting worse. It's basically me, Susan and Gabbi. But Jeff is close enough to be like a brother."

"Yes, he is. And his wife makes the best cookies." Susan nodded to herself.

"I agree with Susan. Sally is a wonderful baker."

A silence spread through the room, but it wasn't awkward. They were just enjoying the food. At least he was. Owen knew how to cook, the spaghetti was wonderful and the company was better. Susan seemed nice and she looked out for her brother just as much as he looked out for her. Sometimes he'd wish he had a brother or sister, but he was happy he didn't. Home life wasn't the best growing up, which was why he'd escaped to the military as soon as he could. There, he'd found the family he'd always craved. Ethan was like a brother, the best friend he'd ever had, and his heart had an empty space from the loss.

"Hey, why the sad face?" Owen's voice broke into his thoughts.

"Sorry, just thinking. You know, when I first saw you, you reminded me of someone. Ethan. He was my best friend, like a brother to me."

"Was?"

"Yeah, he was killed over in Afghanistan. IED."

"IED?" Susan asked.

"An explosive device. He stepped on it. I was injured and sent home. Medical discharge. I'm fine now, but it took a long time to get better. I have my job here and the other guys in my unit."

"So, I reminded you of him?" Owen cocked his head to one side.

"You do. You guys look a bit like each other, not close up, but on the monitors you do."

"Monitors?"

"Ah—yeah. I might have noticed you a few months ago." Harrison coughed into his hand.

"Oh, it's about to get interesting." Susan sat up straighter in her chair.

"You go back to eating." Owen pointed his fork at his sister.

"You're no fun." She stuck her tongue out at her brother.

Harrison chuckled. The interaction between the two was humorous.

"Well, it's my job to notice patterns. You'd been in a few times, you go to the same table and you don't stay long. You could have been casing the place."

"Drew! Yeah, he's an old friend. I go to his table to chat a bit. I'm not a big gambler." Owen shrugged.

"If it wasn't for me noticing the pattern, we probably would have never met. But I'm happy we did."

"Me too." Owen smiled.

Harrison liked it when Owen smiled. He especially liked it when it was directed his way. He wanted to kiss him and see if it tasted like sunshine. It sure brightened his night.

"Aww, how sweet."

"Don't you have somewhere to be?"

"She's fine." Harrison waved away Owen's worry.

"See, Harrison thinks I'm fine." Susan winked at Harrison.

"You're a brat, is what you are."

"But you love me."

"That I do."

"On that note, I am going to go get changed. Harrison, it was wonderful to meet you. I'll see you later, I'm sure." Susan took her plate and glass out to the kitchen.

"You're lucky."

"I know. I try to tell myself that when she is going through something, I have to pull her out of, but all in all, she's a great person. She's moving in here with Gabbi so she can get on her feet and Gabbi has a place to call home. They've moved from place to place a lot and Gabbi needs something permanent."

"It's good you can give them that. Not every brother would."

"She's family." Owen was matter-of-fact.

"But not everyone would see it that way. Too many people wash their hands of family if it becomes too much trouble. I don't see you doing that."

"I can't. It's not who I am." Owen swiped his plate with some bread and took a bite.

"I know and that is what I like about you." Harrison finished up his food and took a nice pull from the bottle of beer.

"I don't think you'd give up on anyone." Owen had picked up his fork and pointed it at him. It seemed to be a thing he did when he talked and ate.

"I'd like to think that. I gave up on my parents, but that is another story. If one of my brothers came to me, I'd be there in a second."

"See."

"This has been nice. I'm happy your sister could be here for dinner."

"Me too."

"She said she was going through a rough patch?"

Owen put down his fork and folded his hands. He looked so serious.

"Yeah. My sister is an alcoholic. She's doing better now. Going to her meetings. She just got kicked out of her last place. We had to move her here in the middle of the night. But she's strong. She's been sober for about a year or so. She just needs a little help, and I'm here. Well, not here. I'm not home a lot, so it makes sense for them to stay here."

Owen Carpenter was a good man. It was nice to know there were good guys left in the dating pool. His luck lately hadn't been the best. Of course, until recently, he hadn't really wanted a relationship. Getting older sucked, but if he could get involved with Owen, it might turn into a nice way to spend the rest of his life.

"I can check and see if the hotel needs staff. Being in Vegas, we have too much turnover."

"That would be great. I've already looked at the station. We don't need anybody right now. I mean, she doesn't have to get a job right away. We've got some savings, but I know she wants to feel like she's helping."

"You guys must have had a great childhood to be so strong."

"We did. My mom was a good cop's wife and my dad was a strong man. We weren't expecting the shootout, but you never do. With Mom, it's been rough seeing her lose herself. I had a hard time putting her in the home, but having a nurse come out just wasn't helping. They didn't always send the same one and I think that made it harder. Now she can keep to a better schedule."

"Man, you are a good boy through and through," Harrison teased.

"Well, I do leave the seat up and sometimes forget to do the dishes," Owen teased back.

"I don't see a problem with the seat, but you did cook, so I can do the dishes." Harrison stood then took his plate to the kitchen.

"That was in no way a hint for you to do the dishes." Owen laughed and picked up his own plate.

Harrison turned to look at him. "I know, but fair is fair." Harrison found the trash can and threw away his beer bottle.

"We can do them together. I think there's a game coming on later. Football. I don't watch a lot of sports, but I remember seeing something."

"I don't really follow teams either. We could watch a movie? I'll have to leave a little later. My guy is coming to install the camera and I want to be there."

"That won't look out of place? You being there when you aren't scheduled to work?" Owen put his plate in the sink and started running the water.

"No, they're used to it. I swear I spend most of my life there. It's nice getting out and actually going somewhere. I've spent too much of my time there, but I love the place and think of it as mine."

"It's good to love what you do, but it isn't anything like the military, is it? Do you miss it?" Owen handed him a washcloth before picking up a towel to dry.

"It is different, but I still have it a little bit with my team at the hotel. I handpicked most of them. I miss it sometimes. Mostly the guys from my unit. I mean, I went from seeing them every day, being in each other's back pockets to not seeing them for at least a month at a time, if they are all in the States." Harrison put a plate in the strainer then reached for a glass in the sink.

Owen started to wrap up the leftovers. "I thought about the military, but I went to college then the police academy." He put the spaghetti in the fridge before wrapping up the salad. "Following in the family's footsteps. I mean, my dad was in the Marines, but only for Vietnam. He had no plans to be in for life. He actually met my mom on leave and went to her house to ask her out. My grandma said no and shut the door in his face. He told her he would be back and he was. They dated for a few months and moved in together. Had a shotgun wedding."

"That sounds wonderful."

"It was. My mom told the story all the time. Now…well, on good days she'll remember it, and I'll tell her the stories."

Harrison was going to go give him a hug when a loud beeping from outside startled him.

"See you boys later!" Susan shouted on her way out.

"Be safe," Owen shouted back.

"Alone at last." Harrison didn't know why he said that. It just tumbled out of his mouth.

Owen turned to look at him. The heat coming off his lover was enough to make Harrison hard. He turned back to the dishes and kept washing. Owen walked up behind him and slipped the pan into the water.

"Why don't we let that soak?" Owen handed Harrison the towel.

"We can finish this first. The anticipation will make it all that much better." Harrison leaned down and brushed his lips against Owen's.

Owen sighed and put his forehead against Harrison's back.

"I know you're right. I'm thinking with my little head."

"I like your little head just fine and I'll like it even more, later."

This time Owen groaned. Harrison smiled and kept washing dishes. Owen began drying them, and together they settled into a small routine. They were finished in no time and the kitchen looked like it hadn't even been used. It seemed Owen was a bit of a neat freak.

"Movie time. I just got cable because of the girls. I'm not sure what channels I have, but we can find something. If not, I have some DVDs." Owen held out his hand and Harrison took it.

He let Owen lead him into the living room and to the couch. They both sat and Owen picked up the remote. He flipped through some channels before clicking on the guide.

"Have you seen that one?" Harrison pointed at some random movie.

He really didn't care what they watched because he didn't plan on finishing the movie. He wanted a bit of quality time before he had to leave for the hotel, and while watching a movie was nice, they would hopefully have plenty of dates later on to just chill with each other. He really wanted to kiss Owen.

Owen looked over at him. "I have."

"Good, let's watch that one." Harrison waited for Owen to set the remote down before he pulled him closer.

For right now, they would snuggle until Harrison just couldn't take it anymore and he attacked Owen. It felt right having the detective in his arms.

Chapter Fifteen

Raymond had finally ditched his grandparents. Dinner had been hell. All his grandpa did was complain. They had no intention of releasing his trust fund yet. They still weren't satisfied that he was on the right path. Whatever that meant.

He made it in time to see the sister get into a car with a bunch of other people.

Fuck.

There was no way he'd be able to take her. Not yet. He'd have to wait for her. He was going to add her to his collection. He'd watched the news and saw that press conference they had put on. Owen had stood front and center. He was leading the task force they were putting together to keep the citizens of Las Vegas safe.

Raymond had to change his plans. He'd go kill the next woman. He'd been waiting for that all day. Maybe afterward he'd pick up a new girl. The women would be more vigilant, at least the locals. He'd be able to pick up a tourist. Maybe he'd go down the strip, far away from the Totally Five Star. The next few he grabbed would have to be far away to keep them from suspecting an inside job.

He wasn't ready to leave yet. He'd killed only one woman. Of course he'd kidnapped eight women and the count was going up. He was afraid just the kidnapping wouldn't be enough to go down in history. He wanted a name like the Hillside Strangler. Something memorable.

He turned his car around and headed for his warehouse. Raymond would spend some time shadowing the sister so he could find a good time to snatch her. He should feel let down that he couldn't take her now, but the promise of watching someone die helped cheer him up.

Raymond took his time driving to his place. He wouldn't rush anything. Sure, he'd already killed, but that one was too easy. She'd just lain there. He wanted more and this time he'd get it. Maybe he should up his game and kill two of them. He'd see how the first one went and go from there. There was no real plan anymore. That had fallen to the wayside after the first murder and it had taken the police longer than it should have to find the body.

Once he got to his place and opened the door, the women talking filtered toward him. They stopped when they heard him enter. The only bad thing about the warehouse was the screeching the door made when he opened it. Everything went silent. It wouldn't be that way soon. He walked into the room with all the cages. Still nothing from the women.

Raymond started walking toward the first cage. "Eenie." Then off to the next. "Meenie." And the next. "Miney." The one next to that. "Mo." He crouched in front of that cage. It just so happened to be the woman he'd taken last from the Totally Five Star. This would do just fine. If he couldn't have the sister, the next best thing would be the woman he'd taken right out from under the cop's nose.

She hadn't been there for the first kill, so she wouldn't be as scared as the others. They'd seen him drag the unconscious woman from the cage and not come back. He wouldn't take her now. He wanted to get suited up. No way was he going to be caught because of DNA. The plan was to drug her, but he kind of wanted the fight. Sure, she'd struggle if she woke up tied to the table, but it wouldn't be the same. Plus it would take too long if he had to wait for her to wake up from the drugs. He needed this *now*.

If he'd known the feeling of complete power he'd feel with kidnapping and killing, he would have started a long time ago. Of course, he might have been caught because he wasn't as mindful when he was younger. Raymond would have to force himself to be cautious now. He was full of pent-up rage from his dinner with his fucking grandparents.

He moved to the sterile room and picked up a pair of gloves. He put them away on the shelf before grabbing his white suit and the blue footies for putting over his shoes. Raymond placed the stuff by the shower. He'd wash off before getting into the suit, but he was being extra careful and kept the gloves on.

Once clean, he suited up, making sure his goggles covered his eyes. No eyelashes or eyebrows would fall on the body. Raymond tucked his hair under the hood attached to the white suit. Everything was standard, no special buys for him that could be easily traced. He did watch crime shows.

Now he was ready for his next kill. This time when he walked into the cage room, all was not quiet. They knew what the suit meant. He unlocked Molli's door. She tried to back away, but he got a good grip on her arm and pulled her out.

"No. Please. Don't hurt me. Money! I have money. I don't want to die. Please."

Raymond tuned her out. Nothing she said really mattered. She was going to die. She even started saying the Lord's Prayer. Like that would help. She almost slipped through his fingers, but he caught her and dragged her to the autopsy table. He'd had to pull some strings to get the thing, but he'd paid cash and worn a disguise when he'd picked it up. People didn't really pay attention so he should be safe. It was a calculated risk.

Strapping her down was difficult. Next time he would drug them before he strapped them down. This time was experience enough. He would be happy just to watch them struggle when they woke up.

He didn't bother gagging her. He wanted the others to hear this time. Raymond finally had her hands and feet strapped in. A little something he'd added to the table.

"Scream all you want, it won't help."

She was babbling to herself now. It was so low he couldn't understand the words. She was still in the dress he'd kidnapped her in. When he ran his hand up her leg, she screamed some more. Raymond had no desire to have sex with her. He was turned on, but it was by what was happening, not by the woman.

"You can't stop me. Pray all you want. You're going to die."

He missed the sensation his touch would have without the gloves, but he wouldn't risk it.

"Open your eyes and scream." Raymond wrapped his hands around her throat and squeezed.

Chapter Sixteen

Owen was having a hard time focusing on the television. Harrison's heart was beating against his ear. When Harrison started running his hands through Owen's hair, Owen was a goner. There was no way he could finish watching the movie. He moved his hands so he could unzip Harrison's pants.

He unbuttoned them and eased his hand inside. Harrison shifted to give him more room, but didn't say a word. He did lift his hips so Owen could push down his pants and boxer briefs. He didn't have enough patience to take them all the way off, but Harrison had room to spread his legs. Owen flipped over and stretched out on the couch so he could take Harrison's cock into his mouth. The position was too awkward, so Owen slipped down off the couch and took off Harrison's shoes and socks before pushing the pants and underwear out of the way.

Now he could have his way with Harrison, who spread his legs wider to give Owen more room. They should take it to the bedroom, but he wanted a taste first. He wrapped his lips around the thick dick in front of him. He hummed as the salty flavor of Harrison crossed his tongue.

Owen closed his eyes and savored the taste. He tugged on Harrison's balls, just enough for him to feel it without hurting him.

"So good, Owen." Harrison had his hands in Owen's hair, running them through it, encouraging him to continue.

It felt good. Harrison could even tug harder if he wanted to, but Owen wasn't going to stop what he was doing to tell him. He went down as far as he could and sucked hard, swallowing around the cock in his throat.

"Too much. Fuck. Owen, I'm — oh yes, right there. Hmm…I'm gonna — soon. Soon."

Owen couldn't have that. He wanted that thick shaft up his ass. He pulled off and kissed the tip of Harrison's dick. He stood up and took Harrison's hand, leading him to the bedroom. He had condoms and lube in there. He'd gone to the store earlier before coming home.

He pushed Harrison down on the bed before taking care of his own shirt, pushing his jeans down, until his shoes got in the way. Owen had to sit on the bed to tug his shoes off. Finally, he was naked. Harrison lay sprawled on the bed, stroking his hand up and down his shaft. He was pinching his nipple with his other hand and watching Owen. He could almost feel the heat from Harrison's stare. It was almost like the first time, but better, because he knew if he licked Harrison's hip, the man would squirm and his breath would catch. It was a sound that really turned Owen on. He crawled up the bed and kissed Harrison's ankle. He didn't stop there but moved up Harrison's body, making sure to stop at his hip and lick his way up until he reached his lover's plump lips.

Owen nibbled on that bottom lip. He was falling in love with the taste of Harrison. He pressed their bodies together. Harrison had to move his hands out of the way. He wrapped them around Owen's body, holding them tight around Owen, like he didn't want to let him go. He could kiss Harrison forever, let the world slip away and forget about his duties.

He swept his tongue into Harrison's mouth. He was home. He shouldn't be, but he was. Right here and now was where he was supposed to be. Still kissing, he got to his knees so he could straddle Harrison, trapping his hard cock between them. Owen could start sucking it again, but he'd have to let go of those lips and he didn't want to.

The two of them broke apart, gasping for air, chests heaving.

"Fuck me, Owen."

"That's my line." Owen leaned over and opened the drawer of his nightstand.

He grabbed the lube and condoms, throwing them on the bed so he could get to them in a second. He ran his hands down Harrison's chest. His lover was so warm. Owen bent down and nibbled at Harrison's throat, balancing himself on his knees and one hand while using the other to open the lube.

"Hand," Owen demanded.

Harrison held out his hand so Owen could get some lube on it.

"Get me ready."

"So demanding." Harrison fingered Owen's ass.

Owen pushed out. He wanted that finger inside him and he got his wish.

"More. Please, Harrison."

Another finger was added and Harrison grazed his prostate. Owen rocked back, but it still wasn't enough. He fumbled until he found the condom then ripped it open. He was going to have to move in order to put it on Harrison. He was reluctant, because those fingers felt so good, but he knew that fat cock would feel even better.

It was a struggle getting the condom on, but once Harrison was covered, Owen took the lube and put a generous amount on Harrison's dick. Harrison was stroking Owen's arm almost too lightly, making Owen shiver. Once he was satisfied that he'd used enough lube, he got back into position and guided Harrison's cock to where it needed to be. He eased down until Harrison was deep inside him.

He let himself adjust to the length of Harrison's penis, his ass on Harrison's thighs. He was so full.

"Owen, for the love of all that is holy—move." Harrison had his hands at Owen's hips, keeping him steady.

Owen nodded and began to move. He arched his back to get a better angle, moving back and forth, up and down, supporting himself with a hand on Harrison's leg and one on his chest. It didn't take long before Harrison had him flipped over with his legs over Harrison's shoulder, pounding into him. All he could do was hold on for the ride. He liked it when Harrison took control.

He arched his back and rolled his hips, keeping in rhythm with Harrison. Owen put his hands on the headboard, pushing back.

"Harrison, yes, yes. Please." Owen licked his lips. "Right there. There. There. Yes."

Owen dug his heels into the mattress, his body tingled from head to foot. He was going to come. He clenched his hole around Harrison's dick. He wanted Harrison to come with him.

"Fuck. Do that again." Harrison panted above him.

Harrison dug his fingers into his hips. If Owen could just reach and grab his own shaft he would come in seconds, but he wasn't sure if he wanted it to end. Harrison rubbed his dick along Owen's prostate nice and slowly, and that was all it took. He didn't even need his hand on his cock, the rub of Harrison's stomach was enough and he was shooting harder than he ever had before.

"Harrison!"

"Soon. Soon. Soon." Harrison chanted above him.

Owen was coming down from his high and had the presence of mind to clutch at Harrison's ass and tap his hole. Harrison howled above him, his whole body going tight, his hips jack-rabbiting as if he had no control. Owen clenched his ass over and over again, pulling Harrison through his orgasm.

Harrison collapsed on top of him. They were both breathing heavily. Harrison was shaking, so Owen wrapped his whole body around Harrison to calm him down. They stayed that way until Harrison's cock slipped out of his body.

"That—"

"Amazing."

"Yeah." Harrison rolled off him and patted his chest.

For a few minutes, the only sound in the room was their heavy breathing slowing until they were lying there, side by side, Harrison's hand still on his chest.

Owen could get used to this. Being in his room with a guy he really liked, coming down from a high that he could get addicted to. Owen didn't really know how much time had passed and he didn't really care. He could stay there forever, but Harrison had a job to do, one that would help Owen in the long run if the killer was attached to the Totally Five Star.

He rolled over and nuzzled into Harrison's side. Just a little cuddle before they had to get back to the real world. The world with killers and kidnappers, the one he was supposed to protect.

Harrison looked over at him. "I should go."

"Probably." Owen snuggled in closer and put his head on Harrison's chest.

"I don't want to." Harrison stroked Owen's back.

"I don't want you to."

"Adulting sucks." Harrison sighed.

"Big ass donkey balls," Owen agreed.

Harrison laughed. It was a good sound. It vibrated through his body and he had to laugh as well.

"Now, where are my clothes?"

"Hmm...good question. They could be in here...or the living room..."

Neither of them moved. It was a few more minutes before something started beeping.

"That's probably Mac telling me he is on his way. I guess I really do have to get up now."

Owen got out of bed and helped Harrison up. It was time for reality to come back for both of them.

"I wish you could spend the night."

"Me too. Maybe next time?" Harrison stood perfectly still waiting for an answer.

"Oh, yes, there will be a next time." Owen walked over to him and pulled him down for a kiss. "And a next and a next. I'm not going anywhere anytime soon."

"Mmm, good to know, but if you don't step away from me, we are going to end up back in bed and that camera won't be installed." Harrison brushed his mouth over Owen's.

"Hopefully we're not going to find anything." Owen laid his head on Harrison's chest. He seemed to be doing that a lot, but he felt like he belonged there.

"I hope not because I really don't want the Totally Five Star in the news associated with kidnapping and murder. I don't know how I'd explain that to the top brass." This time Harrison kissed him on the head as if he couldn't get enough of Owen and Owen was perfectly okay with that.

"Even if we do find something out, it isn't your fault. You're doing what you can to make sure your hotel is safe. They can't ask for more than that."

"But I feel like I've let them down." Harrison slung his arms loosely around Owen's waist.

"You just send them my way. I'll let them know what's what."

"Oh, you will, will you?" Harrison was smiling.

Owen could tell because of his tone. There was no way he could sound like that and not be smiling.

"All right, we need to get you dressed and out of here." Owen patted Harrison's ass and moved out of his arms and around him. He picked up Harrison's clothes on the way to the living room and put them on the couch.

Harrison wasn't far behind. Owen hated to see the clothes go back on.

"Don't look at me like that." His lover slipped the shirt over his head.

"Like what?" He tried for an innocent look, but didn't think it worked.

"Like you want to climb me and screw my brains out." Harrison tugged his pants on, it was a struggle because of how tight they were.

Owen was enjoying the show, but it ended too quickly. All Harrison had left were his socks and shoes. Then he'd be out of the house. Owen knew he wouldn't be gone forever, but he was sad to see him go. Next time he wanted to wake up with Harrison, like back in the hotel. That felt like so long ago and it was only last night.

"Oh, that look. Can't help it." Owen shrugged.

"Remember that thought. Tomorrow?"

"I don't know. It depends on if we find anything. I'm in charge of the task force now, so I might have more time seeing as how I can delegate."

"Call me?"

"I will." Owen patted Harrison's chest. "You call me if you find anything out.

"Is Jeff coming to the hotel tomorrow to do interviews?" Harrison walked toward the door and leaned against it.

"Yes. I'm going to send people to all the hotels. I'm not sure if the others will be as cooperative."

"I'll make sure my people are available."

"Thanks for letting us go through the files."

"We both want this over with."

"Yes, we do." He went up on his tiptoes and brushed a kiss over Harrison's cheek.

"Stay safe." Harrison cupped Owen's cheek and brushed his thumb across it.

"You too." Owen leaned into the kiss. He felt a bit empty when Harrison walked out the door.

He shut the door behind Harrison and put his forehead on it. He stayed that way for a couple minutes before locking up. He turned the porch light on for his sister and went back to bed. He hugged the pillow Harrison had his head on and took a deep breath. It still smelled like him. It wasn't long before he fell asleep and dreamed of the handsome security officer.

Chapter Seventeen

Harrison sat in his car and stared at Owen's house. He'd rather be in there with him, but he'd already set things up to get that damn camera installed. The best thing he could do was leave and get it done. He hoped they didn't catch anything, but his main priority was to keep things on the down-low so his staff didn't catch on.

And didn't that make him feel like shit. He should trust them all, but this freak was on the loose and Harrison had to be vigilant. The people at his hotel *would* be safe. He trusted Owen to do his job, but Owen had to worry about the whole city. Harrison had only one community he had to keep safe.

He started the car and drove back to the hotel. Mac had left a message. He was on his way and would meet Harrison in his office. That wouldn't be an issue because Mac had visited him before. Once he got to the hotel, they could set up the monitoring station in his office then add the camera to the blind spot. He was still trying to figure out why the hotel had such a spot. They had everything accounted for. It really didn't matter now. He was going to fix it and once this whole debacle was over, he'd make sure it was added to the security room.

He had time to think on the drive back and all his mind conjured up were pictures of Owen as he was coming. Harrison would never get tired of that look. And that thing he did with his ass. He wanted that to happen again.

Who knew he could find a guy while in the middle of an investigation into a kidnapping and now murder? Leave it to Harrison to make the simplest things more difficult. He pulled into his parking space and turned off the car. He laid his head on the steering wheel. The only thing he'd change was the investigation, of course. If not for that, he probably wouldn't have met Owen. Life was funny that way.

Now he had to help make it stop. He got out of the car and headed to his office. Mac was sitting in a chair outside his door. He was proud of his staff for not letting him go into the office to wait.

"Hey!" He held out a hand and pulled Mac to him, pounding him on the back. It was good to see him. It had been too long and the next meet-up wasn't for another couple of weeks.

Harrison took his key card, opened his office door and showed him in. Mac stopped to pick up a bag Harrison hadn't seen before. He closed the door behind him.

"What kind of mess did you get into this time?"

"Me? Why does it have to be me?" Harrison threw his hands up in the air.

"Isn't it always you?"

Harrison gave a huff and threw himself into his chair.

"And why do you smell like sex?" Mac crinkled his nose.

"Because I just had some of the best sex of my life, that's why."

"Must not have been too good if you're here and not still with whatever guy you picked up." Mac sat in the other chair and put his bag down beside him.

"That's just it, I didn't pick him up. He is the reason you're here. He's a detective and on a case that lead him here, to the Totally Five Star." Harrison laid his head on his desk.

"See, your mess. I told you."

Harrison waved him off. "I'm just helping."

"Sure."

Harrison sat up and looked at his friend, trying to decide what all he wanted to tell him. Probably everything because that was the kind of friends they were. Of course then all the guys would know because Mac had a big mouth. It would probably be the talk of the next meeting. Such was the life when a group of military men turned into a gaggle of old woman at a knitting circle.

"I noticed him months ago. He comes into the hotel to get a break from his job. I decided to introduce myself last night. We were interrupted when someone was kidnapped from the hotel. Later, we talked about the dead spot we found, which is where you come in." Harrison pointed to Mac. "He invited me over for dinner tonight—with his sister."

"One night and you're already meeting the family?"

"Right? But it was good. I like his sister. I like him. He's a great guy."

"How can you tell?"

Harrison looked right into his friend's eyes. "He would fit in with the group."

"Ah, well, that *is* hard to find."

"I'm not ready to move in with him, but dating, that would be nice."

Mac didn't glance away. They sat like that for a few minutes until Mac spoke.

"You deserve to be happy, Harrison. Now don't fuck it up."

"I told him about Ethan." Harrison hadn't expected to talk about Ethan yet, not with someone he'd just met.

He felt comfortable with Owen and he couldn't explain it. They'd connected. Would he call it love at first sight? No, but it was definitely lust at first sight and they could grow with that. Owen was a decent, strong man who seemed to share at least some of Harrison's ideals. He was hardworking and loyal. The way he was with his family was special. Not many men would stand up like Owen did.

"It is serious."

"Yeah, but—let's talk about it later. Why don't we start setting things up?" Harrison stood from his desk and went back to the table he'd cleared for the system Mac was going to put together.

"Don't think we're done here." Mac got out of his chair and grabbed his bag.

"Wouldn't dream of it. Anything I can do to help?"

"No, it won't take long to put all of this together and after you can take me to where you want the camera setup. Do you have a frequency for the others? I don't want this one to get crossed with the other signal or the secret will be out."

"Yeah, I'll get that for you. Make sure the screen faces away from the door so people coming in can't see it."

"I *have* done this before, Harrison."

"I know, I know."

Harrison stepped back and let Mac do his magic. In no time they were headed out to the blind spot at the back of the hotel. Mac had a couple of small high-powered cameras he mounted so they would be hard to see for someone walking by. Once this was over, Harrison was going to install a visible camera back there.

"All done. Want to get a beer?"

"It's late, but sure, I could use a beer."

"You need anything from your office?"

"No, I'm good."

They walked around the building and headed to a bar that was close by, one they frequented often when he was working late and Mac called wanting to talk. They made it a couple of blocks away when Harrison happened to glance down into a darkened area to see a guy dragging a girl.

"Hey! Stop!" Harrison ran toward them. The man in the hood dropped the body and started running.

"I got him, Har. You get the girl." Mac sprinted past him.

Harrison knelt and checked for a pulse. The woman was alive. He released the breath he hadn't known he was holding. He took his phone out of his pocket and dialed nine-one-one. "I need an ambulance between the Totally Five Star and Rick's. I have an unconscious woman. A man was dragging her down the alley, but we chased him off. The woman is breathing." He hung up the phone after giving the woman's stats. He looked down the way Mac had gone chasing the guy, he tried to remember anything he could about the guy, but it had been too dark.

Mac came jogging back. "I lost him. Damn it. She okay?" He crouched over, his hands on his knees, panting.

"Dude, you need to get back in shape."

Mac flipped him off.

"She's breathing. I think she might have been drugged, but I'm not sure. She fits the profile, so that asshole could have been the kidnapper."

"You going to call your new man?"

"Yeah. The ambulance is on the way, so we should get her out to the street. Did you get a good look at the assailant?"

"At his fleeing back, yeah. It's too dark and he slipped through somewhere. He lost me. He knows his way around this area."

Harrison picked up the woman. He couldn't do too much damage since the man had been dragging her.

"Should you be doing that? You know, picking her up?"

"This isn't a labeled area. The ambulance might miss us. We need to get to the road. When we do, I'll call Owen. Let him know what is happening."

They moved to the street and Harrison laid the woman down on the sidewalk. He sat beside her and got his phone out again. It was time to call Owen.

"Hello?"

Harrison smiled at the groggy voice on the other end. "Hey."

"Oh, hey."

He could picture Owen sitting up in bed, rubbing his eyes, trying to wake up, the blanket pooling on his thighs, cock hard through the sheet. Yeah, he needed to stop thinking like that when he had to tell Owen what had just happened.

"I have some bad news."

"What's going on?" Owen sounded more alert.

"Mac and I were headed for a drink when we saw a guy dragging a woman down an alley. Mac went after him, but he got away."

"The woman?"

"She seems okay, but she's unconscious. We're waiting for an ambulance."

"All right, if I don't get there before the ambulance, call me and let me know what hospital they are taking her to. I'm going to call Polubinsky and get his ass out of bed."

"I'll head up to the hospital if they get here first."

"Stay with her if you can."

"Will do. Bye." Harrison turned off his phone and put it back in his pocket.

"Didn't sound too lovey dovey. You sure you're an item?" Mac bumped their shoulders together.

"When have you ever known me to be all lovey dovey?"

"True, but you could try harder. Make this one count."

"We'll see. It's still new." Harrison folded his hands together and glanced down at them.

Things would have to change on his end if he was going to have a relationship. Right now he had to focus on the case.

"I think this one might be it. I mean, you told him about Ethan." Mac looked over at him.

"A little. Yeah." Harrison shrugged and peered up at Mac.

"We don't talk about Ethan."

"I know. We should. I miss him." Harrison looked back down.

"Me too," Mac whispered.

Ethan might have been his best friend, like a brother to him, but Ethan had been Mac's lover. Sometimes he forgot that.

"Anytime you need to talk, I'm here." Harrison patted Mac's shoulder.

The sirens in the distance broke up their conversation. They would get back to chatting about the past. Harrison would make sure to talk more about Ethan, not just for him, but for Mac. It had been a while since they'd gone out for drinks. They saw each other at the unit meetings, but it wasn't the same.

"After the police talk to you, you can head home or go for that beer. I'll call you later."

"You'd better."

A police car stopped with an ambulance not far behind It. This night was going to drag on forever. Harrison was bone-deep tired. Any euphoria from being with Owen was long gone. He knew the police would want answers, but he really didn't have any, and if he had any hopes of getting in that ambulance with the woman, he was going to have to name drop.

Harrison stood, ready to face the music.

Chapter Eighteen

Raymond ran harder than he had ever run before. Someone was chasing him. This wasn't supposed to happen, not to him. If he wasn't mistaken, one of the guys who caught him red-handed was his boss. Raymond had been careful. His face had been covered. There was no way his boss could have known it was him. None, but he still worried.

He didn't like this feeling at all. He should be on top of the world after his latest kill, but almost getting caught robbed him of the jubilant feeling he'd had before. Now he had only fear. It coursed through his veins. His heart was pumping so fast. He finally slipped away from whoever gave chase. Raymond needed to get back to safety.

Everything had been going great. He hadn't planned on taking another woman. He'd thought about it, but that was all. He'd dumped the body close to the detective's house and driven by the hotel. He just so happened to see the woman strolling along by herself. She fit the profile, so he'd said why not? He parked the van out of the way and walked toward her. He got close enough to put the rag over her mouth and chloroformed her. She'd passed out in no time, and he was dragging her when his boss shouted at him.

The van was finally in view. He'd circled around just in case he was still being followed. He jumped into the driver's seat, shut and locked the door. Raymond gave himself a moment to calm down. He wanted to go home. The warehouse would still be there tomorrow.

On top of that, he had to work tomorrow. Raymond would have to go into his job and pretend nothing happened. He could do this. He was Raymond Freakin' Moore. No one was going to take him down. When he got there, he would keep to his station and not bring attention to himself. It would be business as usual.

No one bothered him on shift. He was friendly, but a loner. It worked in his favor, so tomorrow would be no different.

He started the van and drove home. Raymond rolled down the window, letting the air calm him. It was working, for now. His mind still raced and he couldn't stop thinking about what could have been.

One of the things his grandparents had done for him was get him a nice place outside Vegas. It was a little bit of a drive, but he didn't mind. It gave him time to think. Raymond needed that right now. Too much could have gone wrong and he needed to pick apart what had happened. It could have just been a bit of bad luck. Everything had been going very well. Maybe it was time for a close call. It would keep him on his toes, because there was no way he was going to end up in a small cell and he didn't do needles.

For now, he would focus only on killing. It was what he was getting good at, if he did say so for himself. He would kidnap one more woman, then he would take them all out before starting over with a new batch. Before he grabbed the detective's sister, he would murder one more woman. He would keep the sister until the end. He might even start killing the women in front of the others. Show them what was waiting for them. Raymond could wait for the next batch to do the show-and-tell killing. Well—more show, less tell. That would give him time to move the table into the cage room.

Raymond took a deep breath and another, getting himself under control. Planning helped him. It was just a blip in the road. He knew that at some point someone would see him, which was why he wore the disguise and worked at night. Most people wouldn't think anything of it. It was Vegas. The place with the motto of 'what happens in Vegas, stays in Vegas'. It worked in his favor. Or it had until now. He should have gone farther away from the hotel. Raymond knew better. He was going to have to go to the other side of the strip when he started his new batch.

For now, he would watch the sister and figure out when he'd take her. It would have to be soon, like within the next couple days. Detective Carpenter would be busy with the newest body dump. Too busy to be keeping track of his sister.

He reached his place. There was nothing there that would connect him to the murders and kidnappings. He was careful to keep things very separate. Raymond wasn't stupid. If he wanted to stay out of prison, he had to be smart about things. And getting caught wasn't in the plans.

Maybe it was time to take a breather. He was going back and forth. It was the scare from the possibility of going to prison that had him waffling. It had to stop. He had a plan. He would murder another woman. Get the frustration out of his system. Pick up the detective's sister. Kill the rest.

After work tomorrow, he would head out to the warehouse. Maybe catch some news. See if they found the latest body.

He'd known it would be a long haul. Raymond had to stay the course. The history books were waiting and he was going to be in them. A cautionary tale. He hoped to be one of the biggest unsolved mysteries of all time. People would admire him for getting away with it all in this day and age of digital everything. That would be the mark he left on the world. Hell, he was even going to leave the country for a while, let things cool down then come back. Really throw the police off their game.

Now that he wasn't afraid anymore, the fun of the whole thing was coming back. Before he left, he would find a way to get his money as well. At this point, if he had to, he would kill his grandparents. That fear was leaving him. He was stronger now than before he started his spree, and as long as the money was out of their accounts and hidden, they couldn't touch him. That was the confidence he needed to keep.

Chapter Nineteen

Fuckin' fuck.

How could this evening have turned around on him? Owen had gone to sleep happy. Now he was on the way to the hospital. He'd called Jeff to let him know what was going on, but told him to stay home so he could get some sleep for the interviews tomorrow. Jeff hadn't argued. Not that Owen had expected him to, because if it had been Owen, he would have flipped over and went right back to sleep.

Maybe this would be the break they needed. The kidnapper might not have been caught, but he could have messed up. In the perp's rush, maybe he'd left some DNA behind. Owen wanted this to be over with. One body was enough. He wanted to find the other girls, fast, before the bodies started to pile up.

Time was ticking away. How many more women would be taken and terrified? How was the kidnapper treating them? He worried on that a lot. They still didn't have the forensic evidence back. Hollywood made it all look so easy. It didn't work that way in real life. Hopefully they would have something tomorrow, but he wasn't holding his breath. His case wasn't the only one that needed evidence from the lab. If they caught another body, it might move them up the list, but there was no guarantee.

Owen parked in the lot and went to the front desk to find out where the latest victim was being treated. He flashed his badge and was happy to hear she wasn't in ICU. At least she was lucky enough to have escaped the fate of the others. He hoped she knew how lucky she really was.

When he reached the room, there was an officer sitting outside the door. Owen flashed his badge and went to the door of the room to see Harrison perched on the edge of the bed.

"Hello." Owen knocked on the door frame. He didn't want to startle them by just walking in.

Harrison stood and moved toward him. "Hey, I was just telling Kiki you would be here soon. She woke up a few minutes ago." Harrison turned to the woman. "Kiki Smith, this is Detective Owen Carpenter. He'll take your statement."

"You aren't a cop?" she said to Harrison.

"No, I'm the one who found you." Harrison's voice was gentle, like he didn't want to freak her out.

She started to cry. Her whole body shook. Owen hated to see her cry. It made him think of his sister and niece. The predator needed to be caught. Just seeing this woman break down had him thinking of the other women and what they were enduring.

"Hey now, it'll be okay. You're safe." Harrison moved back to the bed.

Harrison sat on the only chair in the room, but it was close to Kiki. He had a hand on the mattress, but he wasn't touching the victim. Owen thought she would shatter right there, but she seemed to pull herself together.

"Sorry. Sorry." Kiki buried her head in her hands.

"You have nothing to feel sorry about, Ms. Smith."

"Please, call me Kiki."

"Ma'am, Kiki, do you think you could tell me what happened?" Owen went to stand behind Harrison.

Kiki sat up straighter and looked at Owen. It was as if she was seeing right through him as she remembered what had happened. It was eerie as her eyes glazed over and she licked her lips before speaking. Her hands rested in her lap, clenched tightly.

"Yes. Um…I was taking my break and went for a walk. Not too far away because I heard the news report and you know—I was by myself." Kiki shrugged and picked at her blanket. "I thought…I thought, yeah, I can handle this. I got it. Nobody is going to mess with me. I was keeping a good look out 'cause I was told that if you're alert and aware of your surroundings, people would leave you alone. That…that didn't happen. I didn't even see who attacked me. One second I was walking along the sidewalk, the next… God, the next I had something over my face and I was being dragged. I woke up here. I thought it might be some nightmare, ya know?" Tears streamed down Kiki's face, but she wasn't sobbing anymore.

"I'm sorry this happened to you. We're going to do everything we can to get the guy behind this. Is there anything you can remember, like how tall he was? Did he wear cologne? Anything you can remember will help."

Kiki closed her eyes and shook her head. "Nothing. It was so dark. I mean…he might have been a little taller than I am, but not by much. I'm five-six so maybe five-nine. Maybe. I'm not good at that kind of stuff. I make a terrible witness. I'm sorry. So sorry." Kiki was rocking back and forth on the bed.

"Kiki, you did great. You really did. I'm going to leave my card right here on this table. If you think of anything or need something, you call me — day or night. We'll leave the guard here until you're released." Owen hoped that would soothe some of her fears.

"My purse!" Kiki scrambled out of the bed.

"Whoa! It's over there with your other stuff." Harrison held up his hands as if to ward her off.

"Oh, thank goodness. If he had it, he'd know where I live. I couldn't go home. Home is supposed to be safe, you know." Kiki got back into the bed and seemed to deflate.

That was Owen's cue to leave. She would rest up and go on about her life, but now she'd have a fear she hadn't had before. That was the part about the job that sucked, watching innocent people become jaded.

"I'm only a phone call away and the guard is outside your door. You're safe." Owen turned to leave.

"You take care of yourself. I don't have a card on me, but Detective Carpenter can get hold of me."

"Thank you for rescuing me, Harrison."

"You're very welcome." Harrison joined Owen at the door.

Owen gave a nod to the officer on the way out. They walked in silence out to Owen's car.

"You need a ride?"

"Yeah, I rode the ambulance here." Harrison leaned on the vehicle.

"My place?" Owen looked over at Harrison playing with the keys in his hands.

He didn't know why he offered, but it seemed like a good idea. He had been woken up from a nice dream after an even better evening filled with sex. It would be wonderful to go home and relax for the rest of the evening. Maybe have a couple of beers.

"That sounds good. I don't have to be into work until late tomorrow."

"With catching this case tonight, I can go in later too. Jeff will interview your staff in the morning. I have other officers headed to the other hotels." Owen walked to the driver side and got in.

Harrison followed suit and buckled up on the passenger side.

Owen started the car and fiddled with the radio. He shouldn't be nervous. They'd already had a great evening. It was almost going into day two.

"We got the camera installed and hooked up. It's recording now."

"Good. Maybe we'll get lucky and catch a break."

"I'm ready for this to be over and I'm not even on the case. I don't see how you can do this every day. I'm happy I went into the private sector."

"It's hard. That's why I try to take time off and go to the hotel for a little pampering. It takes my mind off things."

"I can see that. I think after this case you might need a whole weekend and I have some vacation time…"

"I like the way you think."

"Hopefully you'll catch the bastard quickly. I can't even imagine what those women must be going through. Watching Kiki tonight really brought it home. It was hard enough seeing that group with the missing friend. You have to catch him, Owen."

"Did you notice anything? Something about the guy that might have stood out to you?"

"Not really. I stopped to help the girl, Mac ran after him, but lost him. Said the guy must know the area pretty well. That's all. I'd say Kiki was right about how tall he is, give or take. He is shorter than you, but not by much. Build-wise, he seemed a little stocky, but that could have been his clothes. He was wearing a hood. His face was in the shadows. I don't think any of us will be much help. Mac saw his fleeing back. Sorry." Harrison shrugged.

Owen put the car in drive and headed to his house. It sucked not having anything to go on. The kidnapper had been right there, in reach of someone being able to detain him, and he'd gotten away. Maybe forensics would get back to Owen tomorrow. The case had moved up in priority once the press conference had been held.

"No need to be sorry. I should be apologizing for interrogating you."

"You're doing your job. I just wish I could help more."

"Being with you helps me. I know that isn't exactly what you meant, but you distract me and I need that from time to time. You're good company and I want to get to know you more."

"Then we're on the same page. I'm ready to find out where we can go." Harrison yawned. "But maybe not right now. Sleep sounds excellent right about now."

"Yeah, I've had a bit more sleep than you have."

Owen's phone rang.

"That can't be good," Harrison said.

Harrison was right, it was about three in the morning. Those kind of calls usually didn't bring about anything pleasant.

"Carpenter."

"This is Jeff. They found another body."

"What?"

"Yeah. Guess where?"

"I really don't want to play guessing games, Polubinsky."

"Two blocks from your place."

"Fuck."

"Where are you? I drove by your place, but didn't see your car."

"I went to the hospital, remember?"

"Right, right. Well, get here."

"See you in a few." Owen hung up the phone.

"What's going on?" Harrison had tilted his body toward Owen.

"We're going to need a rain check. That was Jeff. They found another victim."

"Isn't that kind of soon?"

"It takes three to make a serial killer and a pattern. We just have to keep hoping for some kind of break before more corpses turn up."

"I think I'd rather hear about this on the news than be involved. This just makes it all too real."

"Some days I wish that too. I'll drop you at your place." Owen made a U-turn and headed to Harrison's apartment.

"Is it always like this?"

"No, it's pretty routine to tell you the truth. A lot of paperwork." Some days, Owen liked it boring.

The drive to Harrison's place didn't take long. As much as he enjoyed the company, he had a job to do.

Owen pulled up to the curb and parked the car. He leaned over for a kiss. Harrison met him halfway. It was a light brushing of lips, starting sweet before Owen unclicked his belt buckle so he could get closer.

It was Harrison who broke off the kiss. "You should get to work." He pressed his forehead to Owen's.

"Yes. I should."

Owen knew he should let Harrison out of the car because Owen had a job to do, but the attraction to Harrison made him want to do things that would be considered illegal in a car. Owen nibbled on Harrison's neck, scraping his teeth down the soft skin.

"Owen."

"Harrison. Fuck. I need you."

"We could—" Harrison gestured to the house.

"No time." He reached around Harrison and pulled the lever to get the seat to go back. "This is going to be quick and dirty, but I'm going to taste you."

Harrison fumbled with his pants and took his cock out. Owen swatted his hands away and took that fat dick into his mouth. It tickled the back of his throat, but he sucked as hard as he could, moving his head up and down.

"Owen! Too fast. Fuck. I'm…close. Oh. God. No, shit, Now. Now. Fuck!"

The sounds alone were enough to make Owen want to come, but not yet. Harrison was his priority. He cupped his lover's balls and gave them a light squeeze. That was all it took. Harrison shot down his throat. He swallowed all of that salty goodness. Owen used his tongue to make sure none of Harrison's cum was left. He gently put his lover's cock back into his pants and Harrison zipped up.

"What about you?"

"I get the pleasure of having blue balls. I really hate to suck and run, but I've got to get to that body and back on the case."

"Yeah. God, I want to suck your cock and return the favor."

"Later. Fuck, I want this case to be over." Owen brushed a finger over Harrison's lips, trying not to think of them sucking his dick.

Harrison brought Owen in for a quick, hard meeting of the mouths before getting out of the car.

Owen shifted in his seat, willing his hard-on to go away and waited for Harrison to get inside before heading for the crime scene. He couldn't believe it was by his house. What could that mean? Had the killer seen him on the news and found him somehow? That made the hard-on disappear, because if that were the case, he needed to send his sister and niece to an aunt out in Tucson until the guy was caught. He wouldn't fuck with her safety. Now, to convince her to go. That was going to be the tough part.

Chapter Twenty

Harrison dragged himself out of bed. He wasn't getting much sleep, tossing and turning, wondering if Owen was okay, so he might as well get up and start his day. Seeing a dead body wasn't his idea of a good time and this was the second one in a short period. He'd thought he'd left that behind him when he'd been discharged from the military. He shook his head to get the images of Ethan on the ground, not getting up, half of his body blown to bits, out of his head. That wasn't something he liked to see first thing in the morning.

He stumbled around his kitchen. What he really needed was coffee. Lots and lots of coffee. If he couldn't wake up, he might have to do a lunch nap. Harrison rubbed his eyes before reaching for the coffee container. The *empty* container. *Damn.* He had to go to the store.

For now, he'd have to hope a shower could help him until he could get to the hotel. He might have to have a whole pot. He went to the shower and started the water before he could change his mind and crawl back into bed with the nice, warm bed and the comfy blanket. If

Owen had been there, it would have been a nice morning. That wasn't going to happen, so he had to stop thinking about how wonderful Owen felt in his arms.

After the shower, he pulled the last suit out of his closet and made a mental note to go to the dry cleaner that night and the store too if he wanted to have anything to eat in the house. He really should get himself in order. He was out of everything. Harrison looked around his place. It didn't even appear lived in thanks to all of his time at the hotel. It might be time to decorate the place. Maybe.

The drive to the hotel was over before he knew it. He had to have all the windows down in the car. That helped wake him up more than the shower had. The staff was as polite as always. Every day it was the same thing. "Hello, Mr. Boone. Good morning, Mr. Boone. How was your night, Mr. Boone?" They'd been trained well.

He took the elevator up to the security room. Usually he'd walk, because it was better for him, but all he wanted was a cup of coffee. Stairs would take too long. The ding indicating he'd reached his floor startled him out of his doze.

Harrison wondered how Owen was doing, if he'd gotten *any* sleep. He would have to call him later. Or ask his partner. Unless that was canceled too. A dead body would take precedence over interviews.

And there it was—coffee. The nectar of the gods. Someone had just made a fresh pot. He'd have to thank them later. He poured the heavenly brew and took a sip. He might have even moaned, it was that good.

"I'd let Owen know you're cheating on him—with coffee—but he'd probably join you." Jeff laughed. "It sounds good, though. Can I have a cup?"

"Help yourself." Harrison ignored the other comment to inhale the coffee goodness.

The interviews would go on as planned. He wondered who they'd found, but he was sure Jeff would let him know. He gestured to his office and went inside, leaving the detective to get his coffee. Harrison waited for him at his desk. He would check the camera once Jeff joined him. He didn't expect to find anything, especially with all the commotion last night after the attempted kidnapping.

"This is better than the shit we have at the station." Jeff took another sip of his coffee.

"Happy you like it." Harrison waved Jeff over to a chair.

"I guess the woman they found last night was the one taken from this area the other day."

"Molli?" Harrison sat up straighter in his chair.

"That would be the one."

"Fuck. So there is no order to this unless there are other bodies out there you just haven't found."

"God, I hope not. Two is two too many." Jeff ran a hand down his face.

"I agree. Well, I'm going to set you up in an office for your interviews. Do you want to look at the footage from the new camera?"

"Sounds good."

"I really don't expect to see much on it. Not after the deal last night." Harrison walked over to the monitor and set up the feed from yesterday.

A couple hours later, nothing. Just like he'd expected. Harrison took Jeff to an empty office and gave him a list with the names on it. It would more than likely take most of the day. He went to the kitchen and got a carafe of coffee for the detective to get him through the interviews. He got a nod in return.

Harrison went back to his office. There was never-ending paperwork to do and he had to work up the schedule for next week. It would be a boring morning, but right now he could go for some boring. Later, he'd take a walk around the hotel, maybe hit the gym on his lunch break. Normal everyday stuff.

* * * *

The knock on his door was the only interruption he'd had in hours. He looked up from his computer. Jeff stood in the doorway, arms crossed.

"I'm breaking for lunch. I've got about half of the interviews done. So far we got nada."

"I know that sucks for you, but I'm happy at least half of my people are cleared. I want them all to be. I handpicked most of them. I'd hate to think my judgment was that far off."

"Maybe one of the other guys will have more luck. Or maybe we are off-base on who is doing this. It might not be anyone in the hotels, but that is the only connection we have right now. Could be a local, or hell, even someone here on vacation. Whoever it is, they aren't giving us anything." Jeff threw himself into the visitors' chair.

"You guys will get him. He'll slip up, then I'll be watching news stories saying how he was so nice and people can't believe he was capable of all the bad things he'd done."

"God, I hope so. There was so much different DNA in that alley from last night, I doubt we'll find anything on our guy. He is smart, but we're smarter and we'll catch him."

"Come on, I'll buy you lunch." Harrison got up out of his chair, passed behind Jeff and patted him on the back.

"Deal."

They left his office and Harrison figured now would be a good time to get some insider information about Owen.

"How long have you and Owen been partners?"

"So now *I* get interrogated?" Jeff shook his head.

"Well, I could ask Owen, but you're here."

"It seems like forever, but it's been about ten years or so. He's like a brother to me. My wife loves him more than me."

Harrison laughed.

"Oh, you laugh, but I'm not kidding. She bakes him fucking cookies. What do I get? Nothing. The kids call him Uncle Owen. So yeah, family. Don't fuck with him." Jeff glared at him before smiling. "My duty is done, so now I can stay off the couch. Sally expects you to come to dinner soon."

They reached the hotel restaurant and waited to be seated. He requested a spot out of the way so they could talk. If the case came up, they wouldn't have to worry about someone eavesdropping.

"You don't have to worry about me. We're going to see where it goes. I mean, I already had dinner with his sister."

"Then it's serious for him. Family is everything to Owen."

"I don't have family in town for him to meet, I want this to be serious too. But we've only known each other for a couple days. These things take time."

"Pfft! I told Sally I was going to marry her the day we met. We've been together twenty years now."

"Point taken, but I'm not ready to put a ring on it just yet. I'd like to get to know him better. Take him out when he isn't trying to catch a killer."

The waiter stopped by their table to take their drink order. He was dressed in a white shirt with a black vest and tie that was all very posh, making the restaurant appear extremely upper class, just like all of the Totally Five Star. The staff was very efficient and had their drinks to them in no time then asked what they'd like for lunch.

Harrison had to look at the menu. There were new things on it since they'd gotten their upgrade. There were so many good things for him to choose from.

"I'll have the rotisserie chicken salad and the butternut squash soup." The salad had Granny Smith apples, cranberries, pepitas and goat cheese with the chicken.

"Fruit in your salad? I think that is taking things too far. I'm going to go with a good old steak and potatoes."

What Jeff didn't know about the steak and potatoes meal he'd ordered was it was anything but old. The Totally Five Star had some of the best meat in the city. They had local grass-fed organic beef. It was going to be the best steak Jeff had ever had.

"I like to be adventurous when I eat. You find new things when you travel all over the place. You might like it if you try it." Harrison handed his menu over to the waiter.

"I'll leave that to Sally. I'll stick with what I know. So, what's your story anyway? Military?" Jeff took a sip of his water.

"Yes. After I got out, I didn't know what I wanted to do, so I ended up in security and got the job here. I like the Totally Five Star. It's a good place to work. The organization has been good to me, but I live my job. Might have to change some of that." Harrison fiddled with his glass.

For a long time all he'd needed was his job. After Ethan died and Mac went a little crazy, he'd found solace in the everyday workings of his life. He could keep the hotel safe in a way he couldn't keep his unit safe. He'd even let Mac down. He knew the hell his friend was going through, because he had gone through some of the same, and Ethan had only been his best friend, not a lover.

"Hear ya there. The wife is always on me about my hours, but she does understand. Owen would understand too because — hello, cop. He needs something for himself. He has work and his family. He is the go-to guy when you need something done, but he's lonely. I can see it when he's at my place. And, now don't tell him this, but I really do love him like a brother."

"I won't say a word. It's wonderful that he has you."

"Yes, it is." Jeff smirked.

Jeff seemed like a good guy. And it was nice to see that Owen had someone who had his back. Being a police officer was dangerous. Having loyal people working with him had probably saved his life more than once. That was what a team did for each other.

Their food arrived and they stopped talking to eat. Lunch was great, but that wasn't a surprise since he did eat most of his meals here. He looked around the place. It was just as classy as the rest of the hotel. The theme in here was a bit lighter. More whites and beiges. The chairs were high-backed and cloth, very comfortable. The accents were black and red. High ceilings with more chandeliers hanging down. They didn't do the buffets that the other places on the strip did—not that he minded—it just meant the food was better and prepared to order. The hotel didn't spare expense when it came to food. They were a six-star Michelin restaurant and if the new chef was as good as predicted, they could easily get another star. At night, the biggest and brightest of New York and Hollywood stars dined at the Totally Five Star. Rumor had it the Prince of England and his bride were coming next month to dine.

"Good stuff." Jeff wiped his face with a napkin and put it on the table.

"Almost as good as homemade. Our new chef is one of the best in the country. The Totally Five Star only employ the best and they take pride in their kitchens."

"You say that now, but once you've had my wife's home cooking, you'll never want to come back here. She has the best southern dishes you'll ever taste. She might not be culinary school trained, but her meals comes from years of mom's cooking for their kids."

"I guess I'll have to come to dinner sooner rather than later. I'm all for great food. Owen made me spaghetti last night."

"He cooked for you? You'd better snatch him up. A guy doesn't just cook for anyone."

Harrison threw back his head and laughed. "So you married Sally for her cooking?"

"You tell her that and I will end you." Jeff pointed a finger at him.

Harrison held up his hands. "Okay, okay. Not a word."

"All right. We're good." Jeff went back to his food.

They ended lunch without talk of death and kidnapping. Jeff was a good guy and it was a nice change of pace from his usual lunch at his desk and half an hour in the gym. Now it was back to the grind.

"I'm going to make my rounds, so if I don't see you before I go, I'm sure we'll talk later."

"You've got it and thanks for lunch. I was just going to run out for a burger or something, this was much better."

"You're welcome. Here's hoping you find nothing."

"Bastard." Jeff shook his head and walked away.

Harrison took care of the check then started his walk around the hotel lobby before heading to the casino. He weaved his way through the tables, watching the people gleefully throw away their hard-earned money. Whatever floated their boats. It wasn't something for him, but he didn't begrudge a person their fun. Maybe later he'd go out and have some fun of his own, if Owen was available. Heck, maybe he could talk him into another hotel stay. They both might need a timeout from life.

Chapter Twenty-One

A week had passed. A whole week, and he still hadn't taken the sister. He took a couple days to cool off, but he hadn't had a chance to nab her. She was always with that brat or with too many people. Her schedule wasn't in any type of pattern he could discern.

Raymond was going crazy. It was time to kill another woman to ease the odd ache inside. It shouldn't be that way. Raymond was in control. For this to work, he had to be. It was a stupid plan of a bored person. It wasn't supposed to get personal. Now it was a need and it was getting stronger.

He waited and watched the news. The cops still had nothing, not that it surprised him. They weren't releasing the information about the IDs on the women. Probably keeping it out of the press in case they caught him, which wasn't going to happen. He was careful and his confidence was getting stronger each day. It was time. He had shaken off the near miss last week. His boss had no idea it had been him that night. It had helped him ease the fear of being caught. He was ready.

He was going to relish this one. Take his time and bleed her dry. Raymond didn't think it mattered anymore how he did away with them as long as he included the ID. That was his calling card, not the suffocation like he'd thought. He wanted his third murder to be more dramatic because it put him in the realm of serial killer. The place he wanted to be. He changed his mind about his grandparents too. They were going to die. He just hadn't figured out how yet.

It would be his parting gift to himself. Once he finished off all the women he had in his warehouse and the cop's sister, he would take them out. After that, he would move on. He'd finally figured out how to get to his money and transfer it to a hidden bank account. Raymond would take it all right after he slaughtered them.

If he felt the urge to kill again, he would, but it would be out of the United States where he could hide the bodies. It would add to his count. He still didn't know if he would confess once he was out of range of the law, but he had time. He might not be happy with a media-coined name. That would be his deciding factor.

Raymond gave himself a time frame. If he didn't have the girl in the next week, he would give up on her and work on obliterating the others. He would save the first girl he'd kidnapped for last, as some sort of symbol. He would do one a day. He already had the plane tickets for three weeks from now. It had taken all his savings, but he wouldn't be worrying about money soon enough.

He was done with Las Vegas. Raymond hated it more each day. Every time his grandparents called, he had to fight the urge to kill them. The only thing that stopped him was the fact it would mess up his plans. It was important to stay on track.

It was time to go to work. Raymond hated that as well. It seemed he was full of hate lately. He'd had to do a damn interview last week, but he seemed to pass it. At least he'd held his shit together in front of the cop. It wasn't his boss' boyfriend. Raymond would have liked to have talked to him. To look into the eyes of the man whose life he was going to ruin.

No one would suspect him anyway. Why would a rich boy go around murdering women? He had the answer for that—because he could. It was as good an answer as any.

Raymond couldn't even get excited about the next kill. That was a shame too…because he'd been enjoying it more than he should. The plan again. It was all shot to hell. Maybe he should make a new one.

Hopefully he would get excited about offing one of them tonight. He needed some sort of happiness. Stupid fuckin' woman was messing with his mojo. He wanted her in a cage and bad, but he didn't want to jump the gun. If he messed up again, it would screw with his nerve to keep kidnapping. There was no way he'd beat the serial killer record if he couldn't get it up to take someone. Murdering them seemed to be the easy part. It should scare him, but it didn't. Not anymore.

He had a long way to go to hit any kind of record. Raymond dressed for work and hoped his boss wasn't around. That son of a bitch was moody as hell. Not that he really cared, but when the mood messed with his day, he took notice. That fucker had him doing patrols every few hours. It didn't help his urge to maim. It seemed to be coming at him more and more the longer he waited to dispatch the women.

It would stop tonight. Once he killed again. Then he'd have a couple days of calm. He would use that to snatch the girl. Luck would have to be on his side. It was his time to shine. He knew it. He deserved it.

The phone rang. He walked out without answering it. There was only one person it could be and he wasn't going to let her ramp up his anger anymore. If she did, he might not make it through the day and he really needed to so he could get to his reward. He really, really deserved a reward.

Maybe he'd get lucky and the girl would cross his path. That would make it a good day. No, a great day. He was ready for things to go his way.

Chapter Twenty-Two

Owen glanced down at his phone. It still hadn't rung. Not like it should. He could call Harrison. And it wasn't like they hadn't talked recently, but he still wanted his phone to ring.

"Call him already." Jeff slapped his back and walked back to his desk.

"I will. Later." Owen turned his phone over so he wouldn't look at the screen.

"Why not now?" Jeff picked up some paper from his desk.

"Paperwork."

"It'll still get done. Call him. Invite him to my place for dinner tonight. Sally insists, and if you don't come over, the kids might hold me hostage. Call him."

"We talked a couple nights ago." Owen shrugged.

"So? You can't talk to him again?" Jeff put the paper down and stared at him in disbelief.

"God, stop nagging. I'll do it already."

"Good. You've been an ass to work with." Jeff looked away.

"Yeah, it's been a week since we saw each other. This stupid case is screwing everything up. Gabbi wants me to take her to the mall. Susan is still searching for a job. I haven't seen my mom in a while. Not that she'd notice. And Harrison. How can I miss him this much when we hardly know each other?"

"I don't have the answers. But invite him to dinner and you'll actually get to see him."

"I told you I'd talk to him. I'll see if he can come over. What time?"

"Six-thirty. Be there. Bring wine."

"You know, Sally doesn't care if I bring anything."

"Yes, I do know. The wine is for me. Don't buy that cheap stuff either."

Owen stood and left his desk, taking his phone with him. He really did want to talk to Harrison. He didn't need to wait for Harrison to contact him. He was a big boy. He could get ahold of his lover first. He just hated that they'd only had phone calls. He didn't want to call only to have them not see each other.

The case wasn't going anywhere. There had been no new bodies. No new kidnappings. The forensics reports gave them suffocation as cause of death for the first body, with drugs in her system. She'd probably been asleep when she'd died. The second one, Molli, she'd been awake. Some drugs in her system, but nowhere near what the other girl had had in her bloodstream. Molli. God, he hated that she'd turned up dead. There was no rhyme or reason to the guy. Molli was the last girl the perp had kidnapped and now she was gone. And he hated that he was relieved it wasn't Jade. She might still be out there, alive. He didn't want any of them dead, but he dreaded having to tell that kid his mom had been murdered and hoped it didn't come to pass, but she'd been with the guy the longest. Jade could turn up at any time.

Owen hoped it wasn't the calm before the storm. If it was, things might get shitastic. Maybe the almost-capture had the guy running scared. If that was the case, Owen hoped he stayed dormant long enough for them to find his hidey-hole.

The phone was taunting him and it sounded suspiciously like his partner. Damn Jeff for getting into his head. Owen stopped in a hallway just outside his office, dialed the number and hoped Harrison picked up.

"Hello?" Harrison seemed distracted.

"Hey. It's me. Owen." He leaned against the wall, one foot propped up on it.

"Owen!"

Was that excitement? Owen hoped so.

"Yeah, I was wondering if you could come to dinner with me tonight. With Jeff and Sally."

"Jeff did say his wife was a great cook."

"He wasn't lying."

"Luckily, I'm the boss, so yes, I can come for dinner. Do I need to bring anything?"

"No, I'm going to get some wine to take over. You just need to show up."

"I would really like that. Hold on one second."

There was some shuffling and it sounded like a door closed.

"There. Sorry, I wasn't in my office. I miss you."

"Miss you too. It sucks we've only been able to talk on the phone. It'll be nice to see you."

Another officer walked past him. Owen nodded to him.

"You have the night off?"

"I do. My captain made it mandatory. We need a break before something else happens. You know it will."

"No new leads?"

"Not in the last couple days. It's been a week. Hopefully he doesn't blow up and we find all the bodies." Owen shifted against the wall before putting his foot down.

"Maybe you'll take me up on that massage later."

"I will. Not tonight." Owen hated he'd had to pass on it the first time, but he needed something more right now.

"No. Tonight after dinner you'll be coming to my house so we can fuck like bunnies."

And that right there was what he needed. Owen was happy they were on the same page.

"I like the way you think. I'll bring a bag."

"Good. I'll make sure I have coffee and something for breakfast."

"I'm liking today more and more."

"Me too. I'm very happy you called."

"You know, this is how it might be, if we do this relationship thing. Not always, but there might be times we go weeks without seeing each other. Can you handle that?" Owen worried about the answer. They were so new and it would be so easy to call it quits.

"Owen, I understand about your job. It's one of the reasons I really like you. You're dedicated and loyal. So if you can handle it, so can I."

Owen released the breath he hadn't known he was holding.

"Good. I'm…yeah…that makes me happy." Owen cleared his throat. "We can do this. It'll get better once we get this guy, but there will be times I'll have to put in the hours."

"And we'll get through it. One day at a time, we'll see where it goes."

"Okay. One day at a time. I'll see you tonight."

"Tonight. Bye."

"Bye." Owen hung up the phone.

"What has you grinning like a fool?" Jeff had come around the corner without Owen seeing him.

"Tell Sally she'll have two for dinner." Owen put his phone in his pocket.

"So you called. Nice. 'Bout time. Now stop lurking in the hallways and get back to work."

"Whatever, ass. You were the one who told me to call him."

"Yes, I did, but I didn't tell you to hang out here looking creepy with that big smile."

Owen didn't even bother to sigh because it would give Jeff too much pleasure. Instead, he started whistling, his grin still in place.

"Bastard." Jeff shook his head, but he was smiling too.

With Owen's day looking up, he didn't mind the paperwork. They had a couple small cases to wrap up, then it was back to the kidnapping murderer. Owen was frustrated beyond belief. He wasn't the only one. The whole city was in a panic. It was no way to live.

"This was an accident. You want to write it up and I'll put in the notes for this vehicular manslaughter?"

"Works for me, then we can break for lunch."

"Somewhere greasy."

"Sally got you on a diet again?" Owen took the file Jeff handed over.

"Trying to get my cholesterol down."

"So you really think going to a burger joint will help that?" Owen cocked an eyebrow.

"No, but I want it," Jeff almost whined.

"Don't pout. We can go, but I'm telling Sally."

"You wouldn't. Fuck, who am I kidding? Yes, you will." Jeff sighed "Fine, I have a salad in the fridge."

"Good boy."

"I've got one for you too. Sally said you needed some greens." Jeff's grin was almost evil.

"She does know I don't eat like you do, right?"

"Doesn't matter, I have to go through this, so do you, pal. Plus, you know we've both been eating a lot of crap lately because we haven't had time for much else." Jeff shrugged.

"You don't hear me complaining. I like salad."

"You're a freak."

"You love me anyway."

"I'll never admit it."

Owen made kissy noises at Jeff. That earned him a rubber band to the shoulder.

It helped the frustration level when they could joke with each other. He was one of the lucky ones. Some guys hated their partners, and Owen didn't know how they made it through the day. He had Jeff's back no matter how much he tried to annoy him. Just like Jeff had his. Owen didn't know what he would do if something happened to Jeff, so he just made sure to do his job to keep them both safe.

Tomorrow he would have to go see his mom. It made him anxious not knowing what was going on with her. The home she was in would call him if something happened, but he'd feel better going to see her. Susan had gone a few times, taking Gabbi with her.

He hated the fact that Gabbi was missing out on having a grandparent, but he did what he could to make up for it. So tomorrow, he would take her to the mall. He wasn't the only man on the team anymore. The task force could look after the case.

Maybe he'd take Harrison up on that massage as well. A whole day of family and him. He'd missed too many of his pamper days. He could feel the tension. Some of that would go away tonight while he enjoyed Harrison.

"Stop thinking about sex and get back to work."

Owen blinked, not realizing he'd zoned out.

"What?"

"I can tell what you're thinking about and it isn't the job." Jeff wiggled his eyebrows.

"I can multitask."

"Whatever, that report won't write itself." Jeff pointed to Owen's desk.

"Watch it or I'll tell Sally about the candy bar you had for breakfast."

"You stay away from my wife." This time Jeff wagged his finger at him.

"I can't. She invited me to dinner."

Owen was enjoying the back and forth. The weeks of this case had taken its toll on both of them. They took it to heart and wanted to catch this asshole before more people died.

"Thwarted again. Just get your stuff done so we can eat our rabbit food. I'm getting hungry. Maybe we can have a cheeseburger chaser."

"You're asking for it, buddy."

"Asking for what?" Jeff went back to his notes, barely paying attention anymore.

"A heart attack and probably time on the sofa."

"Yeah, yeah. Back to it, you."

Detective Rita Winchester came up to his desk. "We just caught a body. Fits our guy's MO."

"Shit." Jeff slammed his hand on the desk. "I knew it was too good to be true. Third victim, this makes our guy a serial killer. And as far as we know, he has five more women to take out. Those are the ones we know of."

"For right now, we focus on the ones we know. We can't borrow trouble. Detective Winchester, where was she found?"

"Not too far from where Dr. Harper was found."

That was so very not good. His sister was too close to where these women were being dumped. Was it a coincidence? God, he hoped so. Susan was being safe, but how long would that last? His sister could be reckless and complacent. He'd have to talk her into leaving if that was what it took to keep her safe. He wouldn't worry if she didn't fit the fucking profile. The only thing she had going for her was she didn't work or go to the hotels. Owen would like to keep it that way.

"I don't like that we've had two bodies found so close to your place. It's like the guy is taunting us."

"He thinks he is smarter than us. We've got to catch this fucker." Owen followed Detective Winchester from the precinct. He had to hope there were some clues at the site.

"Guess it's burger on the go. The salad will have to wait."

"I'm still telling Sally."

Chapter Twenty-Three

Harrison was halfway to Jeff's house when he got a call saying the guys would be a bit late. They'd found another body. He had a hard time wrapping his brain around the fact that this psycho could kill people for the fun of it. Who was sick enough to get their rocks off on abducting and killing women?

When he was in the military and had to shoot insurgents, it wasn't fun and games. He did his job and that was it. It sucked. He'd had to come to terms with the fact that he'd taken a life. And watching the caravan blow up in front of him was something he'd never forget. Ethan had been in the lead Hummer. It had been hit the worst. Ethan had been blown apart. There wasn't enough of him to take home.

God, he didn't want to think about this now. It wasn't the time. It was never the time. He should talk to Mac. They'd both watched it happen and neither could stop it.

He pulled up in front of the Polubinsky house. The lights shone in the windows. It looked very homey. He could see why Owen would be lonely after being in a sitcom-style home.

He walked up and knocked. A pretty brunette with hazel eyes opened the door. She had a lovely smile and it made him want to smile back.

"You must be Harrison. I'm Sally. Jeff called and said he'd be late, but you were already on your way. Come on in." Sally stepped aside to let him enter.

"Very nice to meet you, Sally. Owen said not to bring anything, but I doubt he had time to pick up the wine he was bringing so I stopped on my way." Harrison handed over the bottle of chardonnay he'd gotten at the liquor store.

"You didn't have to, but thank you. They aren't that far behind you." Sally turned and walked in the opposite direction.

Harrison followed her to the kitchen.

"Something sure smells good."

"Thank you. It's just some almond chicken with veggies and rice. It should be done soon. I had the kids set the table. If you'd like, you can go sit in the living room and wait."

"If you don't mind, I'll stay here. Is there anything I can do to help?"

"Well, if you don't mind grabbing the big bowl out of that cupboard, that would be great. I'm going to put together a salad to go with dinner." Sally pointed above the fridge.

Harrison got the bowl and set it on the island in the center of the kitchen. It was a great space. Lots of countertops, a big stove and even bigger fridge. It was all done in blues and greens with a splash of white. There was a bar area, and beyond that, a dining room.

If he'd been a chef, he'd have fallen in love with this kitchen.

"Anything else?"

"If you want to help with the salad, I'll check on the chicken. Just pull out any veggies you see in there."

A salad he could do. He went to the fridge. For as much as was shoved in that thing, it was surprisingly organized. Harrison pulled out anything that looked like it could go in a salad. Sally kept a lot of vegetables in that fridge.

Once he had everything on the island, he began washing it. Sally handed him a knife so he chopped the carrots, celery, mushrooms, onions, broccoli, tomatoes and bell peppers. It was shaping up to be a good-looking salad. He threw the lettuce in the big bowl and started tossing the rest of the veggies in.

The door opened and moments later, Owen and Jeff walked in.

"Honey, I'm home!" Jeff yelled.

It was followed by thundering footsteps. He'd wondered where the kids where. In scrambled a boy and a girl, about ten years old. He didn't know Jeff had twins, but then he didn't know a lot about Owen's partner. It looked like he would be fixing that. He could see many nights being spent here with the Polubinskys.

Owen walked over and Harrison opened his arms. It was the most natural thing in the world to hug him tightly.

"Rough day?"

"Very rough day. Another girl. It was him."

"Uncle Owen!" Two tornadoes rushed them.

Harrison let Owen go so the kids could hug him. It looked good on Owen.

"Tabitha and Taylor, this is my friend Harrison."

"Nice to meet you both."

They smiled at him, but didn't say anything.

"Kids, go wash your hands for supper." Sally shooed them away. "Why don't you and Owen wash up and head into the dining room?"

"I can help, Sally." Owen went to the sink and washed his hands.

"I'll help. You go have a seat." Harrison rubbed a hand down Owen's back.

Jeff just rummaged in the fridge and took out a couple beers, then handed one to Owen. He kissed his wife and took the big salad bowl on the way out.

"What do you want me to grab?" Harrison turned to Sally.

"If you take the chicken, I'll grab the rice and carrots. The potholders are on the counter."

Harrison nodded and took the chicken out of the oven so he could carry it to the table. It was just as nice as the kitchen. It had a long table, enough to fit eight. The kids sat at either end of the table so Jeff and Sally could sit together, which was nice because he could sit by Owen.

"What do you want to drink, Harrison?" Sally stood surveying her domain with her hands on hips.

"A beer would be great, if you don't mind."

Sally nodded and went back to the kitchen. She had a couple beers, passed him one and sat.

"Dig in." Sally dished herself some rice and passed it along after putting some on her daughter's plate.

Jeff did the same for his son. Harrison could tell it was something they did at every meal they had together because of how synchronized it was.

Chatter was light, no shop talk. It would be easy for the partners to talk about work, but they kept it away from the table. The kids joined in. Harrison couldn't remember a time he'd experienced something so homey. It was nice. His family didn't talk unless it was to yell. He'd been happy to join the Army. The yelling continued, but it wasn't the same.

Owen took his hand and interlaced their fingers. Harrison could get used to this very fast.

"This tastes amazing, Sally," Harrison complimented the chef.

"Thank you." Sally smiled at him.

"Much healthier than the candy bar Jeff had for breakfast or the cheeseburger he had for lunch." Owen looked at Harrison and winked.

"Hey!" Jeff pointed his fork at Owen.

"What about the salads I sent with you?" Sally looked outraged.

"We didn't have time to eat them. We'll eat them tomorrow. Promise." Jeff glared at Owen.

"Don't look at me that way. I was happy to eat the salad." Owen held up his hands.

"And you wonder why I bake for Owen. Now eat your dinner."

"Yes, ma'am." Jeff saluted Sally.

The kids giggled at their dad, pointing their fingers at him until he pointed back at them.

"That goes for you two as well. Eat up and I'll serve dessert. And not one word out of you, Jeff, or you don't get any."

Owen was smirking. It was like they were two little kids trying to one up each other. And it was wonderful. Almost like he was back joshing around with his unit. It felt like home.

When dinner was finished, they all helped take the dishes into the kitchen, putting them into the dishwasher. Sally made them all go sit back down so she could bring out a cake. She cut everyone a small piece, and they ate it in silence — it was that good.

"I could eat here every night, but then I'd need to be in the gym a couple times a day to keep the weight off. Jeff was right, this is even better than the food at the Totally Five Star and we've got some of the best chefs."

"It's the love." Sally grinned at Harrison.

"I totally believe that. Thank you so much for having me over."

The kids had gone up to bed. Jeff and Owen were tucking them in.

"Well, I had to meet the new man in Owen's life. He's important to us. You're good for him." Sally patted his knee and went to the love seat to sit.

"I hope so. It's new, but we both want something more than we have."

"It takes work, but if you want it, it's worth it," Sally assured him.

"Once this case is over, it'll be easier." Harrison believed that. He really did.

"This thing is eating them both up. Sometimes I wish Jeff wasn't a police officer, but then I realize how much good he is doing. That helps."

"I understand too. I was an MP in the Army. Not really the same, but duty is important."

"It really is, Harrison. I think the two of you can make it." Sally smiled.

Owen and Jeff came down the stairs. Jeff sat next to his wife, and she cuddled into his side. Owen sat next to him. He didn't snuggle in, but sat very close.

If he had to spend an evening with someone other than just Owen, this was the way to do it. Sally and Jeff were a great couple. They complemented each other in a way only twenty years together could do. It was nice to see.

"We've got the day off tomorrow, what are you doing, Owen?" Jeff kissed his wife on the cheek.

"I am visiting my mom and taking Gabbi to the mall. Maybe later, a massage at the Totally Five Star." Owen looked over at Harrison.

"I'm all for that." Harrison agreed.

He would call in the appointment in the morning. A nice relaxing evening.

"Why don't you make spa appointments for me, Jeff?"

"Well, Sally, we have two kids who will one day need a college education, but I think we can spare a bit for a spa day for you. All you have to do is make an appointment, doll face."

"I'll have to take you up on that." Sally patted Jeff's face.

"See what you did, Harrison."

"Don't blame me, Jeff." Harrison shrugged.

"Yeah, don't blame him, treat your wife better." Owen stood and put his hand down for Harrison.

"Listen here, mister, I'll have you know—"

"Yada, yada, yada. We're out of here. Thank you for dinner, Sally. It was good, as always." Owen tugged Harrison toward the love seat.

Owen bent down and gave Sally a kiss.

"See you later, Jeff."

"Sally, Jeff, thanks for having me over. Dinner was wonderful, the company even better."

"Oh, Owen, look at your man schmoozing over here." Jeff chuckled.

"And he does it so well. See you guys later. We can see ourselves out. Don't do anything I wouldn't do." Owen guided Harrison out of the house.

"Shush, go home!" Jeff shouted at their backs.

Owen was laughing and Harrison loved it. It was good to see Owen in good spirits. The last few calls he'd sounded depressed.

"I had Jeff drive. Left my car at the station. Hope you don't mind."

"Not at all. Grab your bag and we'll head to my place."

He waited for Owen to get his stuff before heading to his car.

"I let Susan know I wouldn't be home. Told her to lock up tight. That bastard has been dumping bodies by my house."

"Shit. She fits, doesn't she?" Harrison got his keys out of his pocket and unlocked the door.

"I don't want to think about it. At least not tonight. Make me forget."

"You've got it. You, me and the horizontal tango."

"Sounds like the perfect end to a great evening."

Harrison couldn't agree more.

Chapter Twenty-Four

Raymond walked away from the Totally Five Star. He'd worked the late shift last night so he got to leave early. It was another day of work done. Another day without taking Susan. He'd learned the sister's name. It wasn't too hard to figure out if he hung out at the right place. People didn't really notice him and Raymond used that to his advantage.

He was running out of time. Killing the other woman helped calm him down, but the itch was there in the back of his head, saying he would need to kill again. Soon. He was more clear-headed than before. Either he would get her, or he wouldn't.

The unexpected thing about his path was how much he enjoyed and needed the killing. He had to fight the urge to skip work and head to his warehouse where he could kill the remaining five women.

His van wasn't far away and he trudged through the security dead spot he'd noticed months ago. He was looking down, not really paying attention when he bumped into someone.

No way. It can't be.

But it was. Susan, the detective's sister, was right in front of him. With no one else around.

"I'm sorry. Excuse me." She had a hand on her chest.

"No, pardon me. I wasn't watching where I was going."

She smiled at him. She had no idea that something bad was about to go down. He didn't have his usual supplies with him, but he didn't care. His brain was telling him to take her, screw the consequences, and he was going to listen. He had to get her in his van. It was only a block away. But it was broad daylight and she would put up a fight. There was no way a cop's sister wouldn't know some moves. He had to play it safe.

"You look familiar. Have we met?" Raymond would see if he could get her to come to the van willingly.

"Um...I don't think so."

"Are you going to the Totally Five Star? That might be where I know you from?" Raymond pointed over his shoulder.

"I am. My brother's boyfriend works there. I wanted to ask him something."

"Oh, who is your brother's boyfriend? I might know him."

"Harrison Boone."

"Small world, that's my boss. I'm Raymond, by the way. I work up in security with Mr. Boone, but he isn't up there right now. I don't know if he'll be in today at all." Raymond put his hands in his pocket and tried to look as harmless as possible.

"Well, shoot, I should have called first." She shrugged and turned to head back the way she came. "Thanks." She waved over her shoulder.

"I can walk you to your car." Raymond jogged to catch up with her. She was fast.

"That would be great. You can't be too careful nowadays." Susan slowed down. "I'm Susan."

"Nice to meet you, Susan, and no, you really can't. If you watch the news, there is all kinds of bad stuff happening in the world. Even here, recently. It's awful."

They reached her car, and he opened the door for her to get in. Once she was settled, he leaned down like he was going to say something and slammed her head into the steering wheel. Once, twice, three times, and she was out. He looked around and didn't see anyone. There was no way he would be able to carry her to his van without someone noticing. He'd drive her car and come back for his. It would also let him wipe it down so his DNA wasn't in the car.

Someone up there was watching out for him and gave him the gift of his latest victim. The detective was going to go crazy and there was nothing he could do about it. His sister was going to die, but first he'd play with the good detective. He would kill another woman and use the detective's sister's ID on the body.

Raymond couldn't contain his laughter. He would kill again and he was going to make Susan watch and let her know she would be dying soon.

First he needed to get her to the warehouse before she woke up. It wouldn't do for her to fight back until she was in the cage. Raymond couldn't chance it. Everything had gone the way he'd planned so far. He'd left nothing to be found. Just the body.

He made sure he went the speed limit. He had to be so very careful right now because this was new — kidnapping them and using their own car. He should leave it to be found somewhere. Not at the hotel. He wished he could do that to taunt the cops some more, but there was a good chance someone would see him leaving the car.

The stupid got caught. He wasn't dumb, no matter what his grandparents thought. Fucking grandparents. He couldn't wait until they were dead. He wouldn't take his time with them, they didn't deserve it. They might be worth a shot to the head. That he could do. Maybe with his own grandpappy's gun. That would be justice.

Susan shifted in her seat. He had a few more miles to go. He should have tried to put her in the trunk. It was morning in Vegas, so most people were sleeping off a hangover. He hated the need to be cautious, but he was getting out of the country soon. He had to use his brain and not fuck up.

He had plans. If he had to keep repeating that to himself, he would. It was going the way it should. Sure, he had that itch to kill, but he could control it. It was a side effect he hadn't been expecting, but it would serve his purpose.

God was in the details, at least that was what his grandma always yammered on about. Maybe the only good thing to come from that hag. For him, the details were a god to him. He worshiped them and it kept him safe from capture. Now he'd get to play. Fun for him, not so much for the woman. Too bad. He laughed and kept driving. It was his time. Fuck everyone else.

Chapter Twenty-Five

Owen couldn't believe how lucky he was. He'd finally spent the night with Harrison. No calls interrupted them. They'd both crashed when they got to Harrison's place, but it was all good because they had the day to play. Owen stretched and got out of bed. He found the bathroom and the toothpaste. He'd put his bag in the room last night so he was able to get his toothbrush out without much noise.

He was making his mouth minty fresh when Harrison walked in and put his arms around him.

"Mmph." Owen took the toothbrush out of his mouth and spat into the sink. "Morning."

Harrison nuzzled into his neck. "Well, it was going to be, but someone got out of bed."

"Keep doing that and we'll end up back in bed. I just wanted to clean my teeth." Owen rinsed off his brush and set it on the counter before turning in Harrison's arms.

He laid his head on Harrison's chest and hugged him tightly.

"I could get used to this, Owen."

"Me too." Owen closed his eyes and enjoyed the companionable silence.

Harrison kissed the top of his head before moving aside. He grabbed his toothbrush. Owen watched him. Harrison hadn't bothered with clothes. They'd gone to bed naked the night before.

"I took the day off." Harrison put his toothbrush up. "What do you want to do today?"

"I'm think we stay in bed for a while and enjoy each other. We didn't get to the fucking like bunnies yesterday. We should fix that today. Later, I need to take Gabbi to the mall and if you want, we can go get massages afterward."

"We'll need them if we're going to the mall." Harrison shuddered.

"Gabbi won't take too long. She never does, even when I tell her we can stay. She's an awesome kid."

"I'm not surprised with you as her uncle."

"We've had some rough times, but things are good right now. I think they will be as long as Susan stays with me. It will be nice for Gabbi to have something stable."

"You are a wonderful man, Owen. I don't think I can tell you that enough." Harrison leaned down and brushed their lips together.

Owen moaned and pulled Harrison farther down so he could deepen the kiss. Harrison lifted him. He struggled a bit before realizing he was trying to set Owen on the counter. He let go of Harrison so he could help. Once sitting, he spread his legs so Harrison could step between them.

He barely noticed the chill on the counter. He was too focused on those lips. He could feast for days and never come up for air. Their tongues tangled, but Owen wasn't close enough. He wrapped his legs around Harrison, their cocks brushing against each other's.

Harrison moved away. Owen didn't like that one bit. He might have even whined a little.

"Bed. Now," Harrison panted.

Owen eagerly hopped off the counter and followed Harrison out of the bathroom. His lover had a glorious ass. Owen wanted to take a bite out of it. When they got to the bed, he pushed Harrison down and crawled over his back, pressing him to the bed. He licked a path down Harrison's back, making his way to that delectable butt. He wanted a bite and he was going to have it. There it was, that firm ass. Owen scraped his teeth over one cheek before he nibbled it. He licked the area to soothe it before giving the same treatment to the other globe.

Now that he was there, he was going to do more than bite it. Owen sucked on his finger then rubbed it between Harrison's ass cheeks. It wasn't enough, he was going taste. Harrison got up on his knees, opening himself up for Owen.

He spread Harrison's ass so he could get his face close enough to suck on his pucker.

"Fuck!" Harrison rocked back.

Encouraged, he licked and licked until finally he breached that hole. He couldn't get deep enough. He wanted inside in the worst way, but he didn't want to stop what he was doing. Owen couldn't get enough of Harrison's ass.

"Inside me. Damn, Owen. Now."

Owen felt a dip in the bed. Harrison had somehow manage to toss him a condom and the lube. Owen reached for the lube first. Getting Harrison nice and slick, he eased in a finger, then two.

"You feel so good, I might come as soon as I get inside." Owen scrambled for the condom.

"If you don't hurry, I'm going to come without you. Fuck, you have a talented tongue."

"Wait. Wait." Owen finally got the condom on and eased inside Harrison's hot, tight ass. It squeezed his dick so good. He ran his hands down Harrison's back, not moving yet for fear he'd come.

"Give me a sec." Harrison clutched the sheets, his head hanging down. He was breathing heavily. "Okay. Move." He pushed back.

It was a good thing Harrison was ready because the urge to thrust was overcoming him. Owen gripped Harrison's hips and took him for a ride, pounding him hard. Harrison reached around him and clutched at Owen's ass, urging him onward. Owen picked up the pace, thrusting harder and harder. It was going to be over too fast. He didn't want that, but he might not have a choice. Harrison was so tight wrapped around his cock.

"So. Good. I—fuck, fuck… Oh God, I'm not gonna last." Owen was close.

He slowed down, his body wasn't happy with him, but he wanted a few more minutes to enjoy Harrison under him. Owen bit his lip and did his best not to come, but he couldn't hold out for long. His body was shaking and he had to go faster.

"Soon. Soon. Harder. Come on. Yes! Yes. There, right fuckin' there." Harrison all but howled, his cum coating the sheets.

Once Harrison clenched his ass, Owen was a goner. He came so hard in the condom. He collapsed on top of Harrison, who slid down so he was flat on the bed.

Owen finally got the strength to roll off Harrison.

"Too fast." Owen panted, his hand on his chest.

"No, too good." Harrison moved onto his back, his hands above his head.

"I wanted to take my time." Owen wiggled until he was touching Harrison.

He needed contact. For some reason, he was feeling a bit needy.

"Nap now. Breakfast later." Harrison patted Owen's hip.

"We just woke up," Owen said in disbelief.

"Too early." Harrison threw his arm over his eyes.

Owen laughed. "It's six a.m. This is sleeping in for me."

"Then go make breakfast. Wake me when you're done." Harrison rolled over, his back to Owen.

"So that's how it's gonna be?" Owen sat up.

"Yep." Harrison snuggled under the blankets.

"We should shower. Wash the sheets. Get on with the day."

"Oh, no. You're one of those annoying morning people. That's it, we're through." Harrison ruined it by snorting.

"Just for that—" Owen jumped on Harrison and started tickling him.

"Uncle! Uncle!"

They were both laughing and out of breath for a totally different reason. It was fun, something Owen had been missing in his life. Sure, he could be there for his family, but sometimes he needed more. Something for just him. Or someone, as the case may be.

"Now get up and get in the shower!" Owen slapped Harrison's ass and ran for the bathroom.

Harrison grumbled behind him, but Owen paid him no mind. He got the water started and shoved Harrison into the shower. It wasn't the best fit, but they made it work. He'd thought about giving Harrison a blow job in the shower, but he really didn't have much space so he settled for sudsing up the soap and washing him down, feeling every inch of that skin.

"Mmm, good." Harrison had his hands on the wall, his head hanging down.

Owen wrapped his arms around Harrison so he could get to his chest. He let his hands wander down Harrison's body until he reached his cock. He stroked it a few times before heading for Harrison's balls. He washed them, spending some extra time making sure Harrison was clean.

Harrison turned in his arms and rubbed their bodies together. "All clean."

Owen wiped the water off his face and grinned up at Harrison. "Really?"

"Yep." Harrison took Owen's dick into his hand and stroked. "But I can spend some more time on your extra dirty parts."

"You could rub against me some more. That was nice — and soapy."

He pushed his hand down Harrison's body so he could grab his cock and jack him off. With his other hand, he wrapped it around Harrison's neck and pulled him down for a kiss. He nibbled on Harrison's lips. Owen stood on his tiptoes as sensation rocked his body. Harrison had stopped stroking his cock while they were kissing, but if Owen could get some more friction he would come.

"Harrison, please," Owen whispered against his lover's mouth.

"Kay. Mmm. Owen...close."

Owen nodded and moved his hand faster. Harrison squeezed Owen's dick and that was it.

It should have taken longer for him to come, but he was so turned on it was over. Too fast. Again. He put his head on Harrison's chest. Harrison wasn't far behind him, his body jerking a bit as he orgasmed. Owen held him through it.

The water was starting to get cold and they both began to shiver.

"Breakfast?" Harrison asked as they dried off.

"I thought you were taking a nap."

"Well, we did work up an appetite." Harrison patted his belly.

Owen threw his towel at him. He bent over to rummage through his bag for something to wear. He at least wanted to put on his boxer briefs, especially if they were cooking. No need to burn his bits.

Harrison ran a hand down Owen's ass. It felt nice, but no way was he getting it up again so soon after all the fun they'd just had.

He took his underwear out and put them on before turning to brush a kiss against Harrison's cheek. They made a pit stop in his room so Harrison could put on some boxers, then they headed to the kitchen.

"I picked up some eggs, bread, milk, juice and a bit of fruit." Harrison headed for the fridge.

"Sounds great. I'm starving. What do you want me to do?"

"I'll start on the eggs and if you could do toast, that would be great." He put the eggs on the counter.

It was very domestic. The two of them worked well together. The kitchen was a nice size, not too small or too big. It had enough space that he could make toast without bumping into Harrison making eggs. There were kisses and touches as they fixed breakfast.

The eggs didn't take long. Harrison had scrambled them and added a bit of cheese. He set some milk, salsa, orange juice and fruit on the counter. While Harrison got glasses then dished up the eggs, Owen put the stuff on the table, adding the toast.

They sat to eat. "Mmm, this is good, Harrison."

"Yeah, it's just eggs. Kinda hard to mess up eggs. Not like spaghetti or anything."

Owen laughed. "That is pretty easy to make too. You really just need a can of sauce and to boil noodles."

Harrison shook his head. "If you say so. Eggs is the extent of my talents. Well, that and calling for the kitchen at the hotel to bring something up to my office."

"I'll have to start packing you a lunch. Not that I'm any better. Jeff and I stop at fast-food places all the time."

"You know, he told Sally you guys would eat those salads today, but you're both off work."

Owen had forgotten about that. It was how Jeff wiggled his way out of trouble after eating junk food.

"Ha! I'm going to have to call Sally later." Owen shoveled another bit of eggs into his mouth.

"You two are like brothers." He grinned at his lover.

Owen swallowed and took a drink of juice before answering. "We are and it's great. I always wanted a brother."

"A sister wasn't enough."

"Yeah, but not the same thing." Owen shrugged.

"Ethan was..." Harrison looked down at his plate.

"You know, you don't have to talk about him." He put his hand on top of Harrison's, offering some comfort.

"But I do." Harrison sighed.

"I'm here whenever you're ready." Owen patted his hand and continued eating.

"Ethan was my best friend. You kind of look like him. That's why I did a double take the first time I saw you in the casino. And when you came back—I just had to know who you were."

"Did you two…?"

"No, it was never like that for us. We were brothers. He and Mac were the real deal. Ethan was always there for me and I had his back too. We were friends before Mac joined our unit. We went in together. Then everything went to shit."

Chapter Twenty-Six

Harrison couldn't believe he was talking about Ethan, but he needed to, and Owen should hear about him. Ethan was his best friend and he'd died. It had made a big impact on his life. If he wanted something that would last, it would be a good idea to talk about what would bring him nightmares.

"How so?" Owen tilted his head to the side and gave him a curious look.

It took him a minute to figure out what Owen was asking.

"What? Oh, right, it went to shit. Right. Well we were in Afghanistan on patrol in a caravan. Ethan was in the lead Hummer. It hit an IED. Mac and I were bringing up the rear. I don't remember how we got to Ethan's truck—probably ran—but it's all a blur. We couldn't get to him in time. We tried. Oh God, did we try. We found parts of him. Fuck. It still hurts and haunts my dreams. Seeing him like that—no one should have to see that. I got out shortly after. So did Mac."

Owen moved from his chair and put his arms around him. "I would worry if it didn't hurt. Mac? He's the one who helped with set up the camera?"

Harrison reached up and patted Owen's hand then held on. "Yeah. I don't see him enough. I mean we try to meet at least once a month, those of us who are left. It isn't the same, though. Mac needed his space for a while, but I think it's time for us to talk. Heal. He knows I have his back."

"Everyone grieves in their own time and way. You can always talk to me. I'm here now. Sure, we haven't known each other for long, but I want this to work. I'm in it, just so you know."

"Thanks. I appreciate that and the same goes for me. Now, enough deep talk." Harrison cleared his throat then let go of Owen.

Owen used his thumbs to wipe away the tears Harrison hadn't known he was shedding. Harrison felt lighter than he had in a long time. Maybe the talking thing actually worked and he should do more of it. Pushing down his grief didn't cut it. He missed Ethan and wanted to share him, not only with Owen but with Mac too. Mac needed to move on and find someone to love him, and if Harrison could help with that, he would. Ethan wouldn't want Mac to throw his life away.

"So, who's ready for the mall?" Owen got off his lap and kissed his head.

Harrison groaned. "Isn't Gabbi in school right now?"

"Nope. She did a ditch day. She's a straight-A student, so she needs the break as much as we do. Susan was supposed to call in for her before she left for some errands today. Not sure what she's up to."

"For a police officer, you're a bad influence." Harrison pointed at Owen.

"You'll understand when you meet her. She's too adult for her own good. So I enjoy being a bit bad." Owen grinned at him.

"What time?" He looked over at a clock on the wall. "It's only seven-thirty now."

"I'm going to say around nine."

"Whatever will we do with all that time?" Harrison knew what he wanted to do, but wasn't sure if Owen was up for another round of sex.

He couldn't get enough of his new lover—something he hoped didn't go away anytime soon. Harrison sure was getting it up faster than ever before. He credited it to how sexy Owen was and the chemistry between the two of them.

"I have a few ideas."

"Does it involve handcuffs?" That was a new kink Harrison wanted to explore at some point. Fuck. Having Owen cuff him so he couldn't move and only feel what his lover wanted him to. He was so hard right now he might come from talking alone and that was something that had *never* happened before.

Owen laughed. "You are *not* in luck because I don't have any on me right now." Owen looked down.

Harrison followed his lover's gaze to see the tented boxer shorts. Someone else was just as turned on as he was. It was time for some fun before the dreaded mall.

"Not only are you a bad influence, but you're so unprepared. What if you need to arrest me?"

"Why? You going to do something illegal?" Owen moved closer to Harrison. The words were almost whispered.

"It might be, in some states." Now Harrison was laughing.

This fun was what he'd been missing in his life. The sex was something else. His hand could get a rest. Harrison grabbed for Owen and pulled him close, putting his hands in his lover's boxers so he could squeeze that nice firm, round ass. It was *his* ass and he wanted inside it — now. Laughter was forgotten. Now he could think only about his cock in that ass.

"I'm going to fuck you, Owen."

If Harrison's ears hadn't deceived him, Owen whimpered. It was enough to push Harrison into action. The living room was closer than the bedroom, so he nudged Owen's boxers down to his feet and let him walk out of them before dragging him to the couch. It was about to get a workout.

Harrison sat and Owen crawled into his lap.

"Turn around." As much as he wanted to look at Owen, Harrison was going to take his time, bring Owen to his limits, make him beg for Harrison's dick.

Owen turned on his lap, but Harrison figured out this wasn't what he wanted. No, if he wanted Owen to beg, he had to take it to another level. He stood and put Owen in the position he wanted him in. He needed to get to that ass. He was going to taste it.

"What — ?"

"I changed my mind, Owen. I'm going to eat your ass then I'm going to fuck you so hard you'll feel me for a week."

"Harrison!" Owen hung his head down and braced his arms on the back of the couch.

Harrison got on the floor, leaving his boxers on for now. This was about Owen. He spread his lover's butt cheeks then ran a thumb over the sensitive pucker.

Owen rocked back, just the reaction Harrison had hoped for. Now it was time for his tongue. He ran the tip of it over the hole.

"More. Please." Owen thrust back.

He listened to his detective and pressed harder, letting the tip of his tongue breach his lover's hole as much as it could. Owen was frantic in his movements. Harrison had to take hold of Owen's hips so he could control the action. There was no way Owen was going to come this soon. Harrison breathed on Owen's hole, and his lover shivered.

"I wanna come. Please. Harrison. Pretty please. Baby—I gotta. Please. Please."

One more lick and he was done. Harrison wiped his face. It was time to fuck his lover. He pressed two thumbs into Owen's ass. Alternating one in, one out, stretching it enough to fit his dick inside.

"It's gonna burn."

"I don't fucking care. I need to come. Get inside. Now. Fuck. God. Harrison." Owen was humping the air.

Shit.

Harrison didn't have a goddamned condom. "Don't move." He slapped Owen's ass. "Need a condom. Don't touch yourself." Harrison left the room. He would have chuckled at Owen's groan, but he was too turned on.

While in the room, he grabbed the lube too. It took him seconds to grab what he needed and he rushed back to the living room. He had to pause for a moment to take in the beauty on his couch. Owen was breathing hard and shaking. He'd done that, made Owen so excited the man would probably come the second Harrison was inside him. He couldn't have that.

He moved closer, sliding his hand down Owen's back. Harrison opened the lube and pushed a little inside his lover to ease his way inside. He tossed it away and got his condom on.

"Ready?" Harrison smoothed a hand down Owen's back again.

"God. Yes. Hurry."

Harrison slowly entered Owen's hole. His lover was doing something that was driving Harrison crazy and he wanted this to last a little longer, but with Owen clenching his ass and releasing it, lasting might not be in the cards. He did it over and over, milking Harrison.

He stopped moving, allowing Owen fuck himself on his dick for a second before grabbing his lover's hips, not letting him move.

"Harrison. No. No. No. Let me…oh…oh…please. I need…I need…" Owen ended on a whine.

"It'll be quick."

"Yes." Owen was nodding so hard he almost unseated Harrison.

Harrison laid over Owen's back and gripped the back of the couch so he could thrust hard and fast. Owen couldn't move, he had to take what Harrison gave him.

"Hard."

"Grab your cock."

"Uhnnn."

"That's it. I'm going to take you so hard. Do you feel me? Owen." Harrison was close. He was surprised he could even speak in complete sentences. Owen sure wasn't.

"Owen."

"Yes. Fuck. Yes. Harrison!" Owen's ass tightened as he came.

It took a few seconds for Owen to relax enough so Harrison could keep thrusting. Owen rocked back and that was all it took. Harrison's balls tightened to his body and he was coming — hard.

They both collapsed onto the sofa. Harrison couldn't move. Owen couldn't speak.

* * * *

They were running behind because they'd gone back to bed after the intense lovemaking on the couch. After a brief rest, they needed another shower. Harrison didn't want to meet Gabbi smelling like sex. It was his fault, he wanted Owen's ass and couldn't seem to get enough of it. He'd had more sex recently than he'd had in a really long time. He was going to hurt something if he wasn't careful, but it would be worth it. He looked over at Owen and couldn't keep the smile off of his face. He was happy — very happy — and he had Owen to thank for that. It had been a wonderful week. He could only imagine how it would be in a month. A year. Hell, ten years. He wanted this to work in the worst way.

He hoped Gabbi wasn't upset. He wanted to make a good impression on Owen's niece. He really liked that Owen was so involved in his family. Not many single men would do what he did, inviting his sister and her kid to live with him. Heck, his mom had lived with him for a long time. It impressed Harrison to no end. It was something he wanted. A family. He had his unit, but they only saw each other one day a month, if that. He needed something permanent.

"I'm nervous. More so than when I met your sister."

Owen reached over, put his hand on Harrison's knee and squeezed. "No need to be nervous. She's a kid."

Harrison entwined their fingers. "I haven't been around kids that much."

Well, if you didn't count eighteen-year-olds, the baby soldiers. He'd had to deal with them a time or two. But anything younger had him running the other way and now he was willingly going to a *mall* with a nine-year-old. Not just any nine-year-old, but a girl, the niece of someone he was starting to really care for. It could go so very bad. What did he know about preteen girls? Zip, zilch, nada.

"Gabbi is an old soul. She isn't really girly, but she isn't a tomboy either. She's just...Gabbi." Owen shrugged.

"But she likes the mall?" Harrison took a quick peek at Owen before focusing back on the road.

"Just a couple stores. I figure we can walk around, do what she wants then eat lunch there. Or maybe go somewhere. We can let her decide."

"Which mall are we headed to?"

"I figured we'd hit Meadows Mall. It isn't too far."

They arrived at Owen's place. It was just like he remembered. There were no other cars in the drive so he pulled up and stopped the car.

"Sounds good." Harrison reluctantly let go of Owen's hand.

A girl ran out of the house as Owen was getting out of the car and jumped at him. Like he was expecting it, Owen turned and caught her. It showed a lot of trust for her to let go like that and just know he was going to be there for her.

"Hey, Uncle Owen." She kissed his cheek and he let her down.

"Hey, Gabs. I'm going to put my bag inside, then we can go. Gabbi, this is Harrison. Harrison, Gabbi."

She held out her hand and walked toward him. "Nice to meet you, Harrison."

"Same here. Ready for the mall?"

Gabbi made a face.

"If you don't want to go, we can do something else." Owen headed to the front door.

"Well...I wouldn't mind going to the Disney Store or Hot Topic. If you really don't mind, but I don't want to, like, spend all day there. Too many people." Gabbi followed her uncle.

Harrison leaned against his car and waited for them to come back out. There was no reason for him to follow. Owen was just dropping off his bag.

Seconds later, Owen and Gabbi came out of the house with Owen locking up behind him. It sounded like they were arguing about something on the way to the car.

"I'm getting you a cell phone." Owen opened the car door so Gabbi could get in the backseat.

Harrison got back in the car.

"But Mom —"

"I know your mom thinks you're too young, but you spend time by yourself in a house without a landline. I'll talk to her about it later." Owen waved away her concerns.

Harrison wasn't about to get in the middle of a phone conversation. Nope, he was just the driver. Once he saw they were all buckled up, he started the car and headed to the mall.

"You mean, after you've already bought it and she can't do much about it?"

Harrison watched in the rear-view window as Gabbi gave Owen a look that said, 'Come on, I know what you're doing'. Owen had turned a little in his seat so he could talk to her.

"Yes. But not to defy her. She's your mom and has final say, but this is important. I want you to be safe and having a phone will help with that. I'm not talking some fancy smart thing, just a regular one you can use if you need to."

"Okay, but I still don't think we should do something when she said no." Gabbi sounded like she was giving in.

"To be fair, she didn't say no. She said she wasn't sure."

"I'm pretty sure that's the same thing, Uncle Owen." Gabbi was exasperated and it was coming through loud and clear.

Harrison just shook his head and kept driving. Owen had been right, Gabbi was an old soul who knew what she should and shouldn't be doing. She was also a lot like her uncle Owen.

"Maybe. But like I said, I'll talk to her tonight. I think it is important that you have some form of communication."

"I have the computer," Gabbi was quick to point out.

"True, but it isn't the same thing. Can you dial the police with that?"

"No, but I could send you an email."

"Fair enough, but I'm still getting you one."

"I don't like going against what Mom says."

"And you don't—ever. *I'm* going against it. But just this one thing. Promise. I respect your mother's wishes when it comes to you. I do. But this is a safety issue and once we talk about that, she'll understand. I would talk to her first, but we'll already be at the mall. We might as well pick it up."

It seemed as if Gabbi finally saw the logic in her uncle's words and they appeared to be done talking, so Harrison turned the radio up a little.

They spent most of the morning walking through the mall, stopping when things looked interesting. After lunch, they walked some more. They weren't really stopping at many places and they'd circled around a couple times, but they were having fun talking. Gabbi was a very interesting kid. He liked her.

Owen got her a couple shirts and some sort of stuffed animal thing. And the phone. He ended up getting her a smartphone and she tried to protest, but he did it anyway.

It was better than any other time he'd come to the mall. He might even come back, if he had Gabbi with him. Seeing things through her eyes somehow made things better. He hoped they got to spend more time together.

If his unit could see him now, they wouldn't believe it was him.

They finally went back to the car. It was late afternoon. Harrison was going to drop Owen off at the station to pick up his car. They'd see each other later, but they both had to go back to work tomorrow.

A phone rang. It wasn't his. Owen was patting his pockets, trying to find his. He looked back and Gabbi had hers out, staring at it like it was some foreign object and not a really nice phone. She'd get used to it and maybe it would help her be more of a kid, playing games all the time.

Owen finally found and answered his cell phone. There was a bit of talk that Harrison couldn't hear, then Owen seemed to freeze and began shaking his head.

"No. No. No. No." He dropped the phone to the floor.

"What is it?" Harrison rushed over to him.

"They found another body and she was holding my sister's driver's license."

Chapter Twenty-Seven

Raymond was gleeful. Things were falling into place. He knew he was on the right path and now he felt vindicated in his actions. The body drop had been easy. He figured it helped that he was high on success. Taking her out in front of the others had been a real treat, but it had gone too fast. He'd had a timetable. The next one he would go slow. The screams from the other women had amped up his excitement for the kill. Raymond was ready to do another one right now. He still had five women to take care of now that he'd added Susan. She would still go last. Maybe he'd have her send a goodbye message to her brother. If only he'd be able to watch the cop seeing his sister die. Because, why not? He hadn't videoed any of the deaths. He'd make his own copy to watch over and over again. The plan was getting better as he went along.

The thrill of her waking up in the cage was something he'd always remember. She was going to be fun to destroy. Full of fire. He remembered how the good doctor had been a treat to kill. Watching the anger drain away to fear then the empty stare. He'd gotten hard. A predicament that was becoming more and more prominent the longer he went on. Kidnapping and murder were better than sex. He'd have to think about that later. Maybe. It didn't bother him as much as he thought it would.

He'd gone for dinner after dumping the body and was just pulling into his warehouse space when his phone rang, but he ignored it. It would probably be his grandma and he didn't want her obliterating his buzz. The phone pinged. She'd left a voice mail. He wouldn't listen to that either. Not tonight anyway. He had more women to take care of.

Raymond had made a space in the warehouse so he could actually park in the place so no one would see his car. Always thinking, he was. And steps ahead of the cops, but he didn't want to get too cocky. That would be his downfall.

He couldn't wait to see how his girls were doing. He hoped they were all riled up. He liked listening to them scream and yell at him. A couple of them just whimpered. He might kill them next just on principle. He wanted them to fight. It was something he hadn't expected to like, but now he wanted more.

It was loud when he turned off the car and pushed the button to close the door. It was going to be a wonderful night. He clapped his hands together and rubbed them. He might kill two tonight. Speed things up. Really traumatize the ones who were left. Whatever he did, he was going to enjoy it. It wasn't living unless you were having a great time. For too long he'd just been going through the motions. Not anymore.

Raymond got out of the car, put his keys in his pocket and walked toward the cage room. Susan knelt by the cage door and rattled it then clanged the bars. That box wasn't meant for humans so she didn't have much room to do anything but stay close to the ground. When she saw him come in, she dropped to her ass on the floor and scurried to the back of the cage.

Everything got quiet for a moment as the others noticed he was there. Raymond hadn't bothered to learn their names. No need when they were just going to die. He had no investment in knowing them. There were some exceptions. The good doctor and Susan. They made him notice. Made the thrill of the kill better.

"Hello, ladies. Daddy's home."

The chorus of 'let me out of here' began. But not Susan. She watched him. Her eyes never left him. Raymond walked toward her and knelt in front of the cage.

"How're you doing, Susan?" Raymond banged on the metal bars of the cage.

"Fuck you." Susan's voice quivered.

"Now, now, language." He wagged his finger at her.

"My brother is going to catch you."

"I highly doubt that." Raymond smirked.

This was fun. He'd never talked to the others. He'd thrown them in the room and didn't interact unless he was giving them food or taking their lives.

"You don't know my brother. He's a detective and..."

"I know exactly who Detective Carpenter is." Raymond stood up.

That deflated her vigor. Susan moved closer to the front of the cage.

"Please. I just... Please. I have a daughter. Don't...don't hurt me. Let me go. I won't—"

"Stop. We both know you're lying. I let you go, you run to your brother. I mean, you've seen my face. Don't you watch movies? You see the kidnapper's face, you die."

Susan sat in the center, her arms around her knees, rocking back and forth. She was mumbling something, but he couldn't make it out. He moved closer.

"Praying won't help you. Nothing will. You'd better just come to terms with the fact that you are going to die."

Raymond watched the tears streaming down her face. It was almost a curiosity. It didn't affect him. At all. He had no feelings for the girl. He could stab her right now and *that* he'd feel because it would excite him. But looking at her crying did nothing for him. At least in a sympathetic way.

"You can scream now, if you want." Raymond watched to see what she would do. "Not that it will help, mind you, but you can. No one can hear you out here. Don't worry, I'll save you for last." He patted the cage.

Susan did scream, surged up as much as she could and bit his hand through the cage.

"Son of a bitch." Raymond stepped away from the cage. "Just for that — it's going to hurt. Real bad. You're going to die screaming."

"Let me out of here, you fuckwad. Now." Susan banged against the cage.

"Like I said, scream all you want. It won't change your fate. You will die and I'm going to enjoy every minute of it. Your brother can find your body when I'm done with you." Raymond walked out of the room, the screams of all the woman washing over him.

He went into the room with his tools. They yelled more when he wheeled in the table. He was in control.

They would die and he was going to love every minute of it.

Chapter Twenty-Eight

Owen couldn't believe he'd let this happen. His sister was gone. The fucking bastard had taken her. A serial killer. He'd warned her about keeping safe, but it wasn't enough. He wasn't getting anywhere. Now it was personal.

"Owen, maybe you should go home. Take care of Gabbi. We can stay on top of this." Jeff put his hand on Owen's shoulder.

"I will, but I'm not off this case. I'm catching that fucker before he kills my sister. She's alive, Jeff. I've got to believe it."

"Where is Gabbi now?"

"Harrison is at the house with her. I wanted to check in. Do we have anything?"

"We know he is escalating. Quickly. This last body…" Jeff squeezed his shoulder. "It was bad, Owen. He used a knife. She was alive for most of it. Low level of drugs in her system. The body was clean. The guy isn't giving us anything."

Owen wiped a hand down his face. He was having trouble breathing. This was all wrong. It wasn't supposed to happen to his family. He was pushed down onto a chair, forced to put his head between his legs.

"Breathe. Come on, pal. That's it. Fuck. Don't scare me like that again." Jeff handed him a glass of water.

He sat up and took a drink. "Sorry. This prick is always ahead of us. Someone had to have seen him." He sat the glass down on his desk.

Owen looked around the squad room, but no one was paying him any mind. They were going about their business. Maybe *they* could find something he couldn't.

"We can canvas the hotels again. Kiki was the only one who got close enough and escaped, but she has nothing. We can try questioning her again, but I don't think it'll help." His friend sat on the edge of Owen's desk.

"Everyone and their mother has a cell phone. Why hasn't someone caught him?"

"Good question. Maybe he's local. Knows his way around. Could find the hidden spots in town." Jeff shrugged.

"We haven't found anyone working at the hotels who fits. Unless we missed something."

"This whole thing has been a clusterfuck since the beginning." Jeff crossed his arms over his chest.

"Where is he taking these women?" Owen looked up at Jeff, as if he must have an answer.

"Out in the desert somewhere? I mean, there would have to be noise. Screams. Someone would have reported it by now. Especially after the news conference."

"The guy is a fucking ghost. If we don't find him soon, all the women will be dead. More taken and he'll get away with it. Susan...Susan might already be dead." He slumped down in his chair.

"Stop thinking that way. She isn't dead. Can't be. We'll find her."

"You mean like we've found the other women? We have nothing. It's going to be one of those unsolved cases. On our watch."

"Something has to break. He'll make a mistake. It's human nature. No one is that good."

"Maybe he is."

"Go home. Try to sleep."

"It's so frustrating. I'll go home, but I doubt I'll sleep. I need to be there for Gabbi. God. She was just starting to relax and be a kid. Now this."

Jeff stood. "We are going to do everything we can to get her back. You know this."

Owen stood as well and hugged his partner. "I hope so. God, I hope so."

He walked out of the precinct in a daze. He'd gone to the body drop before making his way to his office. There was nothing there for him. Seeing his sister's driver's license in an evidence bag had almost broken him. Owen had to put on a brave face. His niece didn't need to know her mom might die. He had to give Gabbi hope.

Owen pulled into his driveway without really knowing how he'd gotten there. His thoughts on the what-ifs. He sat in the car for a few minutes, pulling himself together. Susan was his sister, but she was Gabbi's mother. Gabbi needed her mother.

A knock on the car window startled him. He jumped a little and turned to see Harrison standing there. Owen pulled his key out of the ignition and got out of the car. Harrison stepped back so he wasn't hit by the door.

Harrison held his arms open, and Owen didn't hesitate to step into them. Had they only really only known each other a week? It seemed like so much longer.

"Any news?" Harrison rubbed his hands up and down Owen's back.

That tiny bit of affection broke him. He sobbed, letting go like he hadn't allowed himself to do at the station. Harrison was his rock. He didn't say anything, just held Owen and let him get it out of his system.

"Uncle Owen?"

He had to stop. There would be time for him to fall apart later. Well, fall apart more than he already had.

Harrison wiped Owen's eyes and gave him a kiss. "She's been asking for you since you left."

Owen nodded while cradling Harrison's face in his hand. "Okay. I can do this."

"We can do this." Harrison held out a hand. Owen took it.

"Thank you."

They walked to where Gabbi was standing.

"Did you find Mom?"

"I'm sorry, but not yet." He hated the look Gabbi had on her face.

She looked resolved. Gabbi shouldn't have to worry about her mom. Just like Tommy and the families of the other women. He was on the losing team and it sucked.

"You'll find her." His niece stood on her tiptoes and gave Owen a kiss before turning around and going inside.

Owen stumbled back and his lover caught him.

"She has a lot of faith in her uncle."

"God, Harrison. It's…I don't… Fuck. This asshole is ahead of us. We've got nothing." Owen walked into the house.

Gabbi had gone to her bedroom and shut the door. He didn't know if he should go in or leave her alone. Everything was out of his control. Harrison took the choice away from him and led Owen to the couch then pushed him down on it.

"It must be easier in this day and age to get away with more stuff. Think of all the shows on TV and the how-to things on the Internet." Harrison sat next to him.

"We should be able to find him. There is just so much desert out there for him to hide in. Tomorrow they are going to start combing the area."

"You guys are doing everything you can."

"We keep dropping the ball."

"What ball? He hasn't given you much to play with. If he had, you would have caught him."

"How can you have such faith? I understand Gabbi, but you?"

"I've seen the kind of man you are. You live this job and it's eating you up inside not being able to save these women. You're smart and a good cop." Harrison pulled him closer.

"I should be doing something." He laid his head on Harrison's shoulder.

"You are."

"What?" Owen said in disbelief.

"You are here for your niece." Harrison held him tighter.

"Susan should be here with Gabbi."

"We both know that and you'll bring her back."

"God, I hope so."

"I'm here for you." Harrison rubbed his hand down Owen's arm, comforting him.

"Thank you."

It was nice to have someone to lean on. Usually he was the strong one, but right now he could share his burden with Harrison.

"Gabbi is a good kid, you know."

"The best."

Gabbi's door opened and she walked over to the couch, sitting on Owen's other side.

"It'll be okay, Uncle Owen."

"I should be the one telling you that, kiddo."

Gabbi crawled onto his lap and laid her head on his chest. He could be strong for her. Owen would find her mom. That bastard wasn't going to win. Not on his watch.

"I think you needed to hear it."

"I did, thank you, Gabbi. You want to stay home again tomorrow?"

"No. I think it would be best to go to school. Keep my mind off of all this. You know?" Gabbi shrugged.

God, she *was* an old soul.

"Okay. Well, you should head to bed and get some sleep. I'll drive you tomorrow."

"Goodnight, Harrison. Good night, Uncle Owen." Gabbi kissed him and left the room.

"Stay tonight?" He looked over at Harrison.

"Wouldn't be anywhere else."

"Good. I need a beer. What I really need is something stronger, but all I have is beer. You want one?" Owen got off the couch and headed to the kitchen.

"Yeah, I'll take one."

He opened the fridge door, stuck his head inside and stood there. He wondered where his sister was right now. Was she scared? Had he hurt her?

"It won't help."

Owen jumped. He didn't know how long he'd been standing there. He took out two beers and closed the door.

He cleared his throat. "What won't?"

"Thinking about what is going on out there that you can't control. What is happening with Susan. You can be there for her when you get her back. She's going to need you."

"I just can't help thinking about what he might be doing to her. What she is going through. I can't stop it." He handed Harrison a beer and uncapped his. Owen took a big drink. It wasn't what he needed, but he gulped down the rest.

"No, you can't." Harrison took a drink and set it on the counter. "But like I said, you'll be here for her. No matter what."

"He'd better not fucking kill her. I can fix a lot of stuff, but I can't fix dead." Owen dropped his bottle in the trash.

Harrison finished his off, threw it away and held out a hand. "Let's go to bed."

"I won't be able to sleep."

"Who said anything about sleeping?"

"I won't be able to get it up either."

"I could probably challenge you on that, but I wasn't talking about sex. You've got a TV in there. I'm going to hold you and we're going to veg out until we fall asleep."

Owen took Harrison's hand and let him lead him to the bedroom. It might be just what he needed. No pressure, just being held. Owen was exhausted. It had been a long day.

They had crawled into bed, both of them in their boxer briefs, when there was a knock on the bedroom door.

"Uncle Owen?"

"Yes, sweetie?" He didn't get out of bed but looked at the door.

"Can I sleep with you?"

Owen could hear in her voice that she'd been crying, and it was a bit rusty.

"I don't know..." Owen looked over at Harrison.

"I have my sleeping bag." She sounded hopeful.

"Come on in." Harrison nodded at Owen.

The door creaked as it opened, and Gabbi walked in with red, swollen eyes and tear stains on her cheeks.

"We were just going to watch some TV. Any suggestions?" Owen asked as Gabbi spread out her sleeping bag.

"I don't care." Gabbi laid down. "I just couldn't sleep and didn't want to be alone. I'm sorry."

"Don't. Gabbi, don't say sorry. We're here for you. Always." Owen flipped through the channels and found a movie that didn't look too graphic. Some superhero thing he'd seen before. It was easier using it at background noise if he'd seen the show or movie. If it was new he'd pay too much attention and not sleep. It had happened before.

He turned off the light. "Goodnight, Gabbi. I love you."

She didn't say anything. Probably asleep already. That was a relief. Owen hoped she would sleep through the night without nightmares. Hell, he hoped *he* didn't have bad dreams. There was a strong possibility he would. His sister was gone and all he could think about was what she was going through.

Harrison tugged him closer and wrapped his arms around Owen. "I'll be here if the dreams wake you."

This was his new safe place and he didn't ever want to leave it.

Chapter Twenty-Nine

Harrison jerked awake. It took him a moment to figure out what had pulled him out of sleep. Owen was having a nightmare. He'd been expecting it and was happy *he* hadn't had a bad dream of his own. Sure, the kidnapping was nothing like Ethan losing his life, but it brought out strong emotions. And he knew how it felt to lose someone close. He didn't want to see Owen go through that. No one should have to, but it was a fact of life sometimes.

Owen was thrashing and moaning. Gabbi was still sleeping, so he did his best to wake Owen up.

"Owen. You're safe. Shh. Please, Owen." Harrison didn't touch Owen, but whispered in his ear, keeping clear of his body in case Owen woke up swinging.

It was a good thing too because Owen sat straight up. If Harrison had been closer, his nose would have been a goner.

"Wha...where?" Owen looked around and got his bearings. "Oh. Right." He glanced over at Harrison. "Morning."

"You were having a dream."

"Yeah, it was—bad."

"Wanna talk about it?"

"I found Susan. I couldn't get to her. She—"

Gabbi jumped on the bed and rushed her uncle. She was sobbing and holding him tightly. Harrison felt helpless.

"Uncle Owen. I want my mom. You can have the phone back. I don't need it. Please."

This was the first time he'd seen Gabbi act her age. The poor girl shook against her uncle's chest.

"Oh, honey. This is *not* your fault."

"If I had just told you no and we'd gone home—"

"Stop right there. Just stop. The only person to blame for this is the guy who took your mother. And he is going to be sorry he ever did. Do you believe me?" Owen held Gabbi away from him and looked into her eyes.

It was a very intense moment and Harrison didn't know if he should stay or go. "I should—"

"Stay. You should stay. I'll make us breakfast and Gabbi can get ready for school." He untangled himself from Gabbi, gave Harrison a kiss on the check and got out of bed.

Harrison watched him go then turned to Gabbi. "Well, breakfast it is."

"He's very bossy." She had gotten under the covers after her uncle had left the bed.

"He is. It should take a few cups of coffee to be that bossy."

"It's an art form he has perfected." Gabbi nodded.

"I can hear the two of you, you know." Owen peered out of the bathroom.

"I don't think it's a secret, Owen." Harrison chuckled.

"It isn't." She covered her mouth with her hand, holding back a laugh.

Owen pointed his toothbrush at the two of them and went back into the bathroom. Gabbi scrambled out of the bed and headed to the door. She looked back at Harrison.

"You're good for him, you know. Thanks for staying." With that, she left and was back to the strong little girl he was first introduced to.

He heard the shower going and figured he'd get up and stop being lazy. He'd have to take a shower when he got home, but for now, he could use some toothpaste to at least freshen his breath. Today was going to be hard for Owen and Gabbi, but they were strong people and would take the day as it came. He admired that about the both of them.

Harrison ambled into the bathroom and looked for the toothpaste. Owen had left it on the counter. He was in the middle of using his finger to brush his teeth when Owen stepped out of the shower. He looked good wet. And naked. So very naked. Harrison watched in the mirror as Owen dried off. All he could think about was getting back in bed and having his way with the good detective.

It wasn't to be, though. Gabbi needed breakfast before school. He had to get to work and he knew Owen would be back on the case as soon as Gabbi was safely in school. Harrison turned around and made it blatantly obvious he was staring at Owen's body.

Owen glanced up and grinned. "Like what you see?"

Harrison got up close and personal. "I do." He leaned down and kissed Owen, licking at his lips, wanting inside. They might not be able to make love, but kissing—that they could do.

"Mmm." He moaned and deepened the kiss.

Harrison stopped, giving Owen one last press of his lips. "As much as both of us want to continue this, we both know Gabbi needs breakfast before school."

"At least one of us is strong."

"We both know that isn't true. You're one of the strongest men I know." He moved away.

Owen used his towel to dry Harrison off. He wasn't too damp. Owen had already dried himself mostly off when the kiss started.

"Okay, let's go be adults." Owen hugged Harrison close before leaving the bathroom.

Harrison followed him out and found his clothes. Owen was already half dressed. The man was quick. The walked out of the room together, headed toward the kitchen. Gabbi was already there when they walked in.

They didn't have a lot of time so Owen scrambled up some eggs while Harrison made the toast. Gabbi got the juice. It was nice. Very domestic. Harrison liked it. It was something he could get used to and he was happy he had the chance at having a real home.

There weren't many dishes and they cleaned up in no time. Harrison said goodbye to them both and headed home to shower and get ready for his day at the office. Things were getting back to normal after all the interviews. He did have his staff doing more rotations outside the hotel. It made him feel better and he hoped it would keep the kidnapper away from his workplace.

They still had no real idea of who the guy was. It made him nervous and now that Owen's sister was a victim, he had an even greater personal interest. Owen was handling it better than he would have. He'd had a breakdown of sorts, but he'd put on a brave face for his niece.

Harrison didn't take long at his place. Just enough to shower and dress. The morning was already speeding by. He took his turn strolling throughout the hotel. He nodded at Drew and headed to the outside the building. When he reached the place that used to be blind, he looked up at the new camera and remembered he hadn't checked the feed yet today.

He didn't expect to see anything. There hadn't been much activity, which was probably why it was a blind spot. No one expected something to happen right there. He played it back to yesterday.

Was that? No. No. Fuck, no.

Harrison played it back a couple times before he believed what he saw. It was Owen's sister and she was talking to someone. She walked away, and the guy followed and helped her into her car. Then the unexpected happened. The guy reached in and did something before looking around then getting in the car.

He had to play it back five times. The guy was wearing a security uniform. Harrison knew that guy. He paused the video and reached for his phone.

"Owen? It's Harrison. You are not going to believe this. I'm on my way over. Don't leave."

Harrison hung up, not giving Owen time to say anything. He had to make a copy of the video before he could drive over to the station. He looked around the security room and Raymond wasn't there. Harrison couldn't remember if he was on the schedule or not. It didn't matter. He made sure to grab Raymond's personnel file on the way out. Someone how this guy had flown under the radar.

And he wasn't one that people, during television interviews, would say 'But he was a nice guy'. No one really knew him enough to say that. The guy kept to himself and did his job. If he remembered correctly, it had been Raymond's grandparents who had gotten him the job.

The murderer had been under his nose the whole fucking time. The perpetrator had been in his house. Well, it was time to clean up. There would be no more kidnapping on his watch. It was over.

He rushed to his car and all but sped to the precinct. He was lucky he didn't get pulled over before he got there. Harrison raced out of his car, headed inside and stopped at the front desk.

"I'm here to see Detective Carpenter."

The office called back. Harrison didn't have long to wait for Owen.

"What's up?" Owen walked up to him.

Harrison took a moment to just look at the man who was coming to mean so much to him. Right now it wasn't about them. It was about Owen's sister and he had a way to find her. A clue getting them closer to catching Raymond. Fuckin' Raymond!

"Remember when we found the dead zone outside the hotel? And I put up the camera without anyone knowing about it? It paid off. I know who your murderer is." Harrison handed over the flash drive.

Owen looked at the drive in his hand, but it didn't seem as if he was comprehending what Harrison was saying. "Huh?"

"Where's Jeff?" Harrison glanced around.

Owen still seemed a bit dazed. Harrison didn't blame him. His sister was missing and Harrison had the proof they would need to catch the guy.

"At our desk, come on back." Owen was still looking at the flash drive.

Owen managed to lead them back to where Jeff was sitting.

"Owen told me he was ordered not to leave. What's going on?" Jeff tilted back in his chair, his hands behind his head.

"The camera picked up Susan's kidnapping."

Jeff put his chair down and sat up straight.

"This is Susan?" Owen waved the flash drive.

"Yes. She was at the Totally Five Star yesterday for some reason. It'll be hard to watch, but the good thing is that I can ID the guy. He's one of my fucking employees." Harrison threw the folder with Raymond's information on the desk.

Owen sat hard in his chair.

"Hey, I remember talking to this guy. No vibe with him, but he seemed...normal." Jeff shrugged.

"He keeps to himself. No one really knows him. He got the job because his grandparents have some influence. In other words, money. They wanted him to know what real work is. He did his job. That was it. Nothing more, nothing less. Never tried to make friends. Even ate by himself. Usually at the fountain in the hotel."

"Okay, hand it over, let's watch this thing." Jeff held out his hand.

Owen handed over the flash drive. They huddled around Jeff's desk. They watched it a couple times. Harrison was just happy they couldn't see what happened in the car because he was pretty sure Raymond had rendered Susan unconscious.

"Son of a bitch." Owen slammed his hand on the desk. "Where is he?"

"He wasn't at work. I don't think he is scheduled today, but the video should be enough for a warrant, right?" He looked between Jeff and Owen.

"Should be, but with him being careful as he is, I doubt we'll find anything at his place. We need to connect him to some place out of town. We'll run him down. Get a warrant for financials." Jeff was flipping through Raymond's file.

"But if he is careful, will you find anything?" He was beginning to lose some of the hope he had. He knew nothing about procedure. It had to be frustrating for Owen as well.

"We'll have to see what his grandparents own or something through their business. Something *has* to connect him. We have to find this place before he kills those other women." His lover ran a hand through his hair.

"What can I do to help?" Harrison put a hand on Owen's shoulder, showing him some support.

"Nothing. Not yet. We'll talk to his grandparents. Get the warrant. Then we will find the bastard and take him down." Owen squeezed Harrison's hand.

They would take Raymond down. Harrison just hoped they would be in time to save Susan.

Chapter Thirty

Raymond hummed as he put the first woman he'd kidnapped onto the table and strapped her down. Susan was a sobbing mess, rocking back and forth in her cage. Her voice was raw from all the screaming.

He looked over in the corner where the bodies of the other three women were piled. Only two more to go. His schedule was moved up a bit, but that wasn't an issue. The ticket was bought. Tomorrow night, he'd be on his way to Dubai. He had to make a pit stop at his grandparents'. Kill them and transfer all the money to his offshore account.

The woman was waking up. It was showtime. After he was done with her, he'd get Susan to leave a goodbye for her brother and record her death. God, he wished he could be there when Detective Carpenter watched it. Would the detective get as turned on as he would or would he get upset? Cry a little? He should be thanking Raymond for freeing up his life. No more sister to take care of. Too bad Raymond had a type all figured out or he'd take the daughter out as well. How delicious would it be to kill a mother and her daughter? The girl would go first so the mom could watch. It would destroy her even more.

If he had additional time, he'd go back and get her. He had to focus.

"Please."

"I don't know why you're even trying. You know it won't work. Accept your fate."

"My son," she pleaded.

"He'll survive. My parents died when I was young and look how well I turned out."

"God. No." She began fighting.

"This might hurt a bit." Raymond used the scalpel and sliced across the woman's chest.

She stopped struggling against her bonds and screamed. Susan whimpered in her cage. It was wonderful. Music to his ears.

"Oh, Susan, just think, you're next. Soon you'll be yelling from the pain, not just because you're watching. Think about your brother finding your body. Will he be happy you're no longer a burden? Will your daughter start calling him Dad? Do you think she will even miss you?" Raymond made another slice in the other woman's chest.

He liked to keep his lines even. What he was doing now was purely superficial, but he was sure it stung like a bitch. Raymond was enjoying himself. He didn't want to hit anything vital, yet. First he was going to make a nice pattern.

"Now don't move too much and mess up my work." Raymond laughed.

It was freeing for him. He didn't have a care in the world. Just him and the dying woman on his table.

"It won't matter where you go."

"What is that, Susan, dear? Did you say something?"

"My brother *will* find you."

"Why do you care? You'll be dead. And no matter what you take with you to the grave, know this—I *will* get away with this. Your brother is a stupid police officer who can't catch squat. Die knowing I *won*."

He'd cut the woman on his table from the top of her chest to her pelvic bone. It was time for a deeper slice. He'd make it in her leg. He put the scalpel aside and went for the carving knife. He jabbed it into her upper leg until he hit bone. He was going to leave it there. She was begging again. He couldn't tell who was screaming anymore. It didn't matter.

He took the other carving knife he had on his tool table and jammed it into her other leg. He was all about being symmetrical. Now it was time for her arms. More light cuts. Get her used to the pain again before changing it up.

It was fun. He couldn't remember the last time he'd been so happy.

Susan started laughing hysterically.

"What's so funny, dead girl?"

"My brother—"

"Yeah, yeah, you've said it before. I know, he's going to get me. Keep laughing it up, we'll see how you do when I go after you with a knife."

"You don't understand." Susan laughed harder.

It was pissing him off. Raymond needed to take a deep breath and calm down. She wasn't going to ruin this for him.

"What is it that I don't understand?"

"That her brother is right behind you, asshole."

Raymond turned around, knife still in his hand.

"How? It's not possible!" He pointed his blade at Detective Carpenter.

"Drop the knife and get on the ground, motherfucker," the detective yelled.

"No. This can't be happening. I covered my tracks. There is no way you should be here. I had a plan, damn it. You ruined it all!" Raymond screamed.

"I said put it down, asshole."

Raymond waved the blade in the air. "I'm a god. You can't do this to me." He had to calm down. There was a way out of this and he would find it. "You're going to watch your sister die. Then I'm going after the girl. Your niece will fall under my knife and it will be all your fault."

"Bullshit. You're going down. Behind bars for life, if I have my way."

The detective was edging closer to him, his gun drawn. It couldn't go this way. They were stupid, and *he* was the smart one. If anyone was going to die today, it would be the detective. He could get him with the knife and make a run for it. He had a couple escape routes in the warehouse. Raymond charged Detective Carpenter.

He heard the shots—one, two, three. He didn't feel them at first. The bullets jerked his body, but he kept moving forward until he collapsed. It was his turn to scream.

"You aren't taking me alive." Raymond raised the knife.

Another shot rent the air. It hurt his hand. Nothing was going right. This was his path. It had been working so well. How had they found him? His vision started going dark and he hurt so badly, but he was alive. He tried to get the knife that had been dislodged from his hand, but he couldn't find it. If he couldn't escape, he had to die. The surge of adrenaline had him more aware. He thought he was going to pass out, but that had gone away. He had to get them to kill him.

"You're not going to die. Not yet, you bastard. I'm thinking death row is the perfect place for you. Now stay down. Jeff, you got him?"

Raymond was rolled to his back, his hands dragged behind him.

"I was going to gut your sister. Listen to her scream. No worries, I was gonna record it for you."

"Owen, go help your sister. You and I both know what this fucker is trying to do. It's not happening."

Raymond was dragged to his feet. He didn't like Detective Carpenter's partner. "Kill me."

"I'm sure you showed the same mercy to *your* victims. Let's go." The partner dragged him out of the warehouse.

He was fucked.

Chapter Thirty-One

Owen collapsed in front of the cage his sister was in. She had come to the front, her fingers through the little bars. He was crying. She was crying. No way was he waiting for a key.

"Honey, I need you to move back. I'm going to shoot this lock off. Cover your head, okay? That's it. This is going to be loud." Owen stood and aimed true. The loud clang echoed in the room and the lock opened.

He threw open the door. Susan scrambled out and jumped at him. He caught her and hugged her tightly.

"Owen, help her." Susan pointed in the general direction of the other victim.

"I will. Are you okay?"

"No. No, I'm really not, but I haven't been stabbed. Go." Susan sat on the floor. "Just—help her. I'm out of the cage. I'll be fine. Just fine." She put her face in her hands and her shoulders shook.

It took everything he had to leave his sister on the concrete, but they had a victim who could bleed out. On his way to the table, he saw the other three bodies.

The fucker had already killed them. Out of the nine women, only two had survived. If he didn't help the other woman, it might only be one survivor.

Owen hated thinking how grateful he was his sister had not been touched. It could be her in that pile of corpses. He'd have nightmares about it for months. He got to the table. The naked woman had been strapped down. Superficial wounds crisscrossed her chest. The ones he was worried about were in her legs. The knives were still there.

"Hey, there. I'm Detective Carpenter. You can call me Owen. I'm going to get you out of these restraints, okay? The ambulance is outside. What's your name?"

"I...I...my name." She dragged in some air. "Jade. I'm Jade."

"You don't know how happy I am to see you. I met Tommy. He's a good kid who will be happy his mom is home."

She started sobbing hysterically and he couldn't understand what she was saying, but he didn't need to. She was alive and would be going home to see her son. He wouldn't have to tell that little boy his mom was dead.

The paramedics were there with a stretcher. Jeff had called a couple ambulances out because they didn't know what they would find. It was a good thing they had.

"The other ambulance took off with Mr. Moore. Your sister can go with—"

"Jade."

"The girl with the kid?"

"That would be the one."

"At least that's two things that went right. Fuck. We'll have to call in someone to pick up the bodies. Forensics is going to have a field day with this place." Jeff had his hands on his hips as he surveyed the scene.

"We can leave them to it. I'm going to have to turn in my weapon, then I'll follow the ambulance."

"I'm with you. There's a tech over there." Jeff pointed to a man standing with a kit by one of the cages.

His sister was being checked over. He went over to her. "They're going to take you to the hospital. I'll be right behind you."

"Gabbi?"

"She's at school. Once we get you settled, I'll go pick her up." Owen bent down so he could kiss her on the forehead. "I need to go talk to one of the techs, but I will be there when you're checked in."

She reached for his hand and squeezed. It took a moment for her to let go. Owen didn't blame her, because he didn't want to let her out of his sight again. He was sure she would get tired of him hovering, but she'd have to put up with it for a little bit. He'd almost lost her.

"Hey, I'm Detective Owen Carpenter. I fired my weapon and shot our suspect. I'm handing it over until the investigation clears it. I'll file my report later. I'm following my sister to the hospital." Owen pointed to where the paramedic was taking his sister out of the door.

"Let me get a bag." The tech reached into the kit on the floor and grabbed a bag then opened it for him.

Owen put his gun in and waited for it to be sealed. They both signed it into evidence. He was free now to follow his sister. She might not have been under the knife, but he'd noticed her busted lip and bruised nose. That asshole must have hit her in the car. If he could shoot him again, he would. Raymond Moore was unlucky in that Owen was a good shot. He wanted Raymond to suffer and an easy death wouldn't do the job.

The ambulance was getting ready to pull away. He could see his sister sitting on the bench, Jade on the stretcher. The doors closed and it was off. Jeff was waiting at the car.

"Everything situated?"

"They have my weapon, the bastard is under guard on the way to the hospital and Jade and Susan are alive. I'll count that as a win. So, yeah, I'm as situated as I'm going to be right now." Owen climbed into the car.

He needed to call Harrison. He got back out of the car.

"What are you doing?"

"You drive. I want to call Harrison."

They switched places and Jeff started the car then followed the ambulance. Owen called his boyfriend. He liked the way that sounded.

"Boone here."

"Hey, Harrison."

"Owen! What happened?"

"We found the warehouse. The psychopath killed three of the women. Susan was okay. Well, as okay as she could be locked into a dog cage. Jade, a woman with a little boy, she was on a table. It was bad, but she was alive when she left."

"And Raymond?"

"I shot him a couple times, but he'll live."

That was hard to say. As much as he wanted Raymond to suffer through a court case and imprisonment, the thought of him dead made Owen happy.

"I can hear your disappointment over the phone."

"I wanted to kill him, but that would have been too good for him. I want him behind bars. Plus, it might look bad if he was riddled full of holes with my sister being one of his victims. I had to be on the up and up. Not that I wouldn't be no matter what, but I won't say I wasn't tempted."

"He'll have some good attorneys. He has money and comes across as sane."

"Depends on if his grandparents will support him. They might not once they get the whole story. We talked to them earlier. They were shocked, but the grandfather seemed resolved once the shock wore off."

"Yeah, but he is still family."

"True, but we caught him red-handed. He was over the body with a knife in his hand. We have two witnesses. It's an open-and-shut case."

"I hope so. It'll be good to have this behind us. I am so happy your sister is safe."

"God, me too, and I agree, I'm very happy this part is over. I wish we'd gotten there sooner, but I can't let that get to me. We're on the way to the hospital. They're going to check my sister out and I want to see how Jade is doing. I promised Susan I'd bring Gabbi to see her."

"If you call the school, I'll go pick her up and bring her to you."

"You have to work."

"Perks of being the boss. I told you, I'm here for you. This is me, being here for you."

"I'm not going to argue. We'll be at Centennial Hills."

"We won't be far behind."

"Thank you."

"See you soon." Harrison disconnected the call.

Owen looked at the phone and realized just how lucky he was.

"Harrison is going to bring Gabbi to the hospital." Owen put his phone back in his pocket.

"Good, I'll drop you off and head back to the precinct and start the reports."

"Thanks."

"Harrison isn't the only one there for you, buddy. I've got your back."

"Yeah, I know. I love ya, man."

"Now don't be getting all mushy on me."

"Never!" Owen laughed.

He made a quick call to the school and set it up so Harrison could take Gabbi out of class. A big burden had been lifted from his shoulders. They'd caught the bad guy. His sister was safe. Maybe now he'd get a good night's sleep, if he could get the image of those bodies out of his head. That was one of the fucked-up things about his job. He'd be forced to go to a few counseling sessions. It was mandatory for an officer-involved shooting.

He wasn't too good to turn down help. Some guys tried to be all macho and say they didn't need it, but that wasn't Owen. He wanted to talk about it, get it off his chest so he could move on. He didn't regret shooting Raymond. What he did regret was not finding him sooner. That guilt would eat at him and he couldn't let it.

"We're here." Jeff had pulled into the ER while he'd been lost in thought.

"I'll call you later. Give you an update."

"You'll have to come in. I'll hold them off for tonight. I'll see you sometime tomorrow. Bring your sister in and we'll make it official. We can talk to Jade once she is on the rebound. We'll have enough to keep an officer on Raymond for the duration just because of what we saw. We'll make this airtight."

Owen slapped Jeff's shoulder. "Thanks." He got out of the car and waved Jeff off.

He walked in and went to the desk. A tired-looking woman sat sitting behind a computer. The area didn't look too busy.

"Hello, I'm Detective Carpenter. My sister, Susan Carpenter, was brought in along with Jade Chase. Another ambulance brought in a Raymond Moore. He should have an officer with him at all times."

The woman punched a few buttons on her keyboard. "Your sister was moved to a room upstairs. They just want to monitor her for the night. Ms. Chase is in surgery and so is Mr. Moore. There was an officer with him when he was brought in. I can't tell you much more until they are out of surgery."

The nurse gave him the room number for his sister. He texted Harrison the number and headed up. His sister was so still. It was hard to see her this way, but not as hard as seeing her in that cage.

Susan turned her head toward the door. When she saw him, she smiled. "Hey, you."

"Hey." Owen walked into the room and pulled a chair up to the bed so he could hold her hand.

"I knew you'd come. I even told that monster you'd catch him."

"Gabbi had faith too."

"Is she here?" Susan let go of his hand so she could sit up. She smoothed the sheets in a nervous gesture.

"No, not yet. I called the school. Harrison is bringing her so I don't have to leave you."

"All I could think about was how she'd grow up without me. For a minute I was thinking she might be better off, but—"

"Don't ever think that. Gabbi needs you."

"She's had to be the adult for so long, but that changes, now." Susan wiped the tears off her face.

"Sis, I love you. You're a good mom. Sure you've had some ups and downs, but you're steady now. And I'm always here for you."

"Thank you for that. If not for you, I don't know where I would be right now."

"So, why were you at the Totally Five Star?"

"I was going to see about a job. I ran into that monster and…well, you know the rest. It was—oh, Owen, it was so horrible. He…he…God, he killed those women in front of us."

Owen hugged her tightly. He didn't want to ever let go.

Chapter Thirty-Two

Harrison had one happy girl on his hands. Once he'd told Gabbi her mom was safe and with her uncle, she'd been all smiles. It was good to see after yesterday's nightmare. Harrison never wanted to go through something like that again. No one should have to go through what the Carpenters had gone through. They'd probably be in therapy for years.

Now that the case was over, he would have to get Owen to the hotel spa. He'd make appointments for them all. A family spa day was something they could all use. Hopefully Susan would be able to go to the Totally Five Star after her incident. If she couldn't, they could go to another place. As much as he loved the hotel, he wouldn't want to make Susan uncomfortable.

They walked up to the hospital and took the elevator up to the floor Susan was on. It didn't take them long to find the room. When they got to Susan's room, she lay dozing in the bed. Owen sat in a chair watching his sister breathe.

The look of love on Owen's face was something to treasure. It was one of the reasons he was falling so hard for the good detective. He had such a big heart and he was so loyal to his family.

Owen must have heard something. He jumped out of the chair so fast he stumbled.

"Uncle Owen!" Gabbi rushed her uncle.

"Shh. Your mom is sleeping."

"No, she's not." Susan sat up in bed.

Harrison stood back by the door and watched the family reunite. He didn't stay there for long—Owen motioned for him to come closer. The met in the middle of the room, away from the bed to give Gabbi and Susan time to talk.

"Thanks for bringing Gabbi. I really didn't want to leave Susan." Owen moved closer.

Harrison opened his arms. Owen collapsed into his chest.

"No more thanking me. I was happy to do it." Harrison kissed the top of Owen's head.

"Just so you know, I'm going to have a meltdown soon."

"I'll be here when you do. I was just thinking we all need something relaxing. If your sister doesn't want to go to the Totally Five Star, we can find a different place, but I think we all need some down time after all of this."

"I couldn't agree more. We have to go to the station tomorrow to give a statement. You'll need to give an official one as well. Then we can forget about this until the trial. Well, depending on what the media picks up, but we can ignore it. That's what cable is for."

Harrison shook his head and laughed. At least Owen was in good spirits for now. Everything was going to hit him soon. Harrison hoped Owen could wait until they were alone to let go.

Susan was talking to her daughter. Gabbi was animated like he'd never seen her before.

"Oh, he did, did he?" She looked over at Owen.

"Uh-oh, I think she just found out about that phone, Uncle Owen. You'd better go fess up."

Owen tugged Harrison with him. They walked up to the bed.

"Mom, he said it was for safety."

"And she needed a smartphone for that?" She glared, but she was also smiling, taking away some of the sting.

"Well…"

Owen was blushing. Harrison wouldn't have believed it if he didn't see it for himself.

"That's what I thought. But I am happy she has the phone. Thanks, Owen."

"Yeah, thanks, Uncle Owen."

"That's what an uncle is for, right, Harrison?" Owen winked at him.

"If you say so." *This is what family should be.* Harrison enjoyed watching the three of them interact.

A nurse walked into the room. "I'm afraid visiting hours are over and the patient needs her rest."

"Uncle Owen, I want to stay here with Mom." Gabbi looked distressed at the idea of leaving.

Harrison didn't blame her. Gabbi had thought she might never see her mother again. They were all going to be in protective mode for a while.

"I'd sleep better if she was here." Susan all but pleaded.

"We can't have all of you staying." The nurse looked at Owen.

"I'm going to put an officer outside her door. Harrison and I will leave and be back in the morning. How does that sound?" Owen lifted an eyebrow.

"That should be fine." The nurse checked Susan's vitals, noted something on the chart and left the room.

"Try to get some sleep, you two." His lover walked over and gave his sister and niece kisses.

"Thank you for bringing Gabbi." Susan gave Harrison a big smile.

"Anytime."

Gabbi rushed over and gave him a hug. "I'll see you later?"

"You sure will." Harrison hugged her back.

They didn't say much as they headed to Harrison's car. It was a comfortable silence. He was waiting for Owen to fall apart. He could do it now that Gabbi and Susan were both safe.

"I feel like I can breathe again. You know?"

"I can imagine. I'm just happy this is over and you have your family back."

"I hope you're counting yourself in that. God, Harrison, you've been a rock and I can't thank you enough for helping catch this guy."

"I'm just sorry we didn't get him before he took your sister in the first place."

"Me too. But we can't fix that. As much as I want to second-guess myself, I can't let the guilt bring me down. I'd be no good to anyone if I did."

They reached Harrison's car and were soon headed away from the hospital.

"Where am I going?" Harrison glanced over at Owen before looking back at the road.

"My place. Can you stay?"

"I can. I told them I was taking the day off tomorrow. They were shocked and asked what had happened to their boss, but all in good fun. They just aren't used to me taking time. They now want to meet you and thank you for giving me a life."

Owen laughed. "We should probably go by your place first so you can get some clothes, maybe a toothbrush."

"Excellent idea." Harrison changed lanes and adjusted his course.

"You know, we could just stay at your place."

"We could, but your place is a tad closer to the hospital. It won't take me long to get some stuff together."

"Maybe." Owen cleared his throat. "Um, maybe you should bring enough for a few days?"

"Yeah, I can do that. The girls won't mind?"

"No, they've been telling me for a while to get a life, kind of like your employees. Well, I've got one now so they'll have to deal with it. I have a feeling we'll want to stay close for the unforeseeable future. Can you deal with that?"

"You don't see me running away, do you?" Harrison parked his car, unbuckled his belt and leaned closer to Owen. "I'm in this. We might have only met a week ago, but I feel like I've known you forever. I'm falling for you — hard. We already agreed to see where this is going. I see me in it for the long haul." He kissed Owen to bring his point home.

"Not running. Got it. Me either." Owen rested his forehead against Harrison's.

"We'll get through this and help your sister through the trial. She's going to need help. I can't imagine the horrors she has witnessed."

"She told me he made them watch as he killed the others. No one should witness that. We need to make her safe."

"We can do that. I'll stay at your place as long as you need me to so she isn't alone until she is ready. I'm not here for just you, I'm here for your family too. I think Gabbi stole my heart."

"She's going to have to give it back, because it needs to be reserved for me." Owen rubbed his thumb over Harrison's lips.

It was a gesture he was quickly becoming addicted to.

"Let me go up and get my stuff. You want to wait in the car?"

"No, I'll come up with you. I think—I think I'm coming down from my adrenaline high. I need to get out of this car." Owen scrambled out.

Harrison was quick to follow. He opened the door and ushered Owen inside. Once they crossed the threshold, Owen headed for the couch and began rocking.

"What can I do?"

"Hold me? God, I sound pathetic."

"No, Owen, you sound like a guy who had to live through someone kidnapping his sister. A man who thought his sister was dead. The one who found those other dead women. I'd be worried if you weren't breaking a little." Harrison threw his keys on the table and moved so he could take Owen into his arms.

Harrison held on tight. Owen was shaking, his whole body vibrating.

"If we would have shown up any later, they would have all been dead. If not for you, I wouldn't have my sister."

"Stop thinking 'what if'."

"I— Yeah, I should. I will. It isn't rational in my mind yet. We were so close. I talked to Jeff while we waited for you and Gabbi. Raymond had a flight booked for Dubai. He would have been in the wind."

"Has anyone talked to him? Asked him why?"

"Not yet. He was in recovery and not awake. We'll send one of the task force members out to get his statement."

"Not you?" Harrison looked at Owen in disbelief.

He thought for sure Owen would want to be involved.

"Conflict of interests. Don't get me wrong, I'd love to be there, but I'm not fucking anything up. I don't need to see him again until he is on the stand. I'll read the report."

They sat on the sofa with Harrison holding Owen tightly. If this is what Owen needed, it was what he would get. They had all the time in the world. Tomorrow would come soon enough and they would have to deal with the real world. For now, they could take comfort in each other.

Owen was fast falling asleep.

"Come on." Harrison stood and reached down for Owen. "You're beat. We'll stay here and go to your place in the morning, like you suggested. Let's get you to bed."

Owen nodded and followed. He stood there while Harrison undressed them both. This is what it meant to have someone in your life who was just for you. He would be the rock when Owen needed it and he knew Owen would be there for him if he needed it. They were on the road to forever, one step at a time. There was no need to rush. And he'd meant what he'd said about Owen's sister and niece, they were quickly becoming family for him. Gabbi would have him wrapped around her finger in no time. She never expected much and it made him want to give her everything.

He tucked Owen into bed before locking the front door and turning off the lights. Harrison walked back into his room and watched Owen sleep. Tomorrow would bring a long day of hospital discharge and police reports, but right now, he was going to crawl into bed with the man who was quickly stealing his heart and dream of the day they would always be going to bed together. The time for that would come quick enough. Tonight he was going to cuddle his lover and hope to keep the bad dreams at bay.

Owen shifted and curled into his chest. He mumbled something before settling back to sleep.

"Sweet dreams, Owen Carpenter. I'll be here when you wake up." Harrison kissed the side of Owen's head.

It was time for him to sleep and dream of the future. Tomorrow would get here soon enough and with it, a new life with more than the hotel to keep him warm. For all the horrors this day had brought, it had also given him a family. He'd count himself lucky to be a member of the Carpenter clan. They wouldn't be able to get rid of him now. He smiled down at Owen and drifted to sleep.

Bring on tomorrow, I'm ready.

Epilogue

One year later

There had been no trial for Raymond Moore. He'd made a plea deal to escape the death penalty. Owen was good with that. He'd rather Raymond rot in jail than get the easy out death would give him. And it was easier on Susan. He didn't want her to relive the events any more than she had to. The dreams were enough. Many a night, he'd woken up to her blood-curdling screams. As far as he knew, Susan hadn't had many nightmares lately. They talked about it when she needed a shoulder to lean on.

Owen's sister had settled in nicely at the house. So much so that a few months into dating Harrison, they'd got a place down the street and moved in together, leaving Gabbi and Susan the old place. She'd gotten a job in the kitchen at the Totally Five Star and seemed to be on a stable road. He was happy for her. Gabbi was still a little adult, but he and Harrison spoiled her whenever they could.

His mother didn't know any of them on most days, but he still made sure to see her once a week. More if he could swing it. Harrison had taken to stopping by sometimes too. It warmed his heart how much his lover fit into his family. And how much he fit into Harrison's life. He'd gone to one of the monthly meetups with Harrison's unit, and Mac was a frequent visitor in their home.

And a month ago, Harrison had proposed. It had been a great night with dinner out. They'd both had some time off. Owen didn't spend the night at the hotel anymore, neither did Harrison. Not when they had each other to come home to, but they did like the spa. Probably more than they should, but there was no way he was giving it up. Harrison had taken him to dinner after his massage and proposed in the restaurant. Of course Owen had said yes.

Now he was standing in front of a mirror adjusting his bowtie. A tuxedo. He would have been happy to put on a Hawaiian shirt. They *were* getting married in the Graceland Wedding Chapel. *Elvis all the way, baby.*

"Are you sure? I mean, you could wait. Make it a bigger deal." Susan stood behind him and brushed off his shoulders then straightened his jacket down his arms.

"I like the place. Harrison liked the place too, and how can you get married in Vegas and *not* have the King do the service? They have the nice gazebo for pictures. The place is small and intimate. Family and close friends only. You're lucky I'm in a monkey suit. I opted for khakis and Hawaiian shirts."

Gabbi chose that moment to walk in. She was so cute in her tux. She was his best 'man'. He told her she could wear a dress, but she opted for the tux.

"It's time to go, Uncle Owen."

"You are just too cute for words." Susan turned to her daughter.

"Aw, Mom. Stop." Gabbi blushed.

"She's right, kiddo, you look great!" He grabbed his niece and gave her a hug.

"Hey! Watch the hair." She pulled away and brushed her fingers through her hair. She looked in the mirror and fiddled with her locks a bit before turning to glare at Owen. She had it slicked back in some style he'd never seen before, but it suited her.

His phone beeped, letting Owen know he had a text message.

You ready to do this?

More than ready.

I'm on my way. Goin' to the chapel and we're gonna get married.

xoxoxoxo

Missed you last night

Missed you too.

We'll make up for it tonight.

Owen smiled at the screen before put his phone away and followed Gabbi and Susan out of the house. He'd stayed the night with his sister. It was a silly tradition, but one he wanted to follow. They might be getting married at a wedding chapel on the strip, but there were some things he didn't want to leave out.

It was already going to be somewhat of a bittersweet day. His mom just wasn't well enough to come. He'd discussed it with her nurse, but they'd both decided it just wasn't going to work. It would be stressful for her and Owen didn't want to make her uncomfortable. He had his sister and niece as well as his partner and his brood. Harrison had invited his unit. Mac was his best man. That was all they really needed. They would all go back to their house after the ceremony for some cake, then it was off to the hotel. Harrison had gotten them the honeymoon suite at the Totally Five Star. It was a good thing he got an employee discount.

Hell, Mr. Sosa had practically given them the room. They'd managed to keep the bad press down for the hotel. Sure, Raymond had worked there, but he hadn't just taken women from the Totally Five Star. It had been hard for Harrison to hire someone to take the killer's place. He'd questioned his judgment, but it was getting better.

They arrived at the chapel. They'd decided they didn't really need a limo, but they were totally having the Elvis experience. They only planned on doing this once and wanted to make it as fun as possible. The trick would be getting everyone to dance at the end of the ceremony.

Harrison was waiting by the door for him with Mac. People were headed into the chapel. It was close to time for them to exchange vows. Owen thought he'd be nervous. It was a big step. One that he wouldn't have taken if his marriage wouldn't be legal everywhere. Looking at Harrison calmed him. He'd been his rock for a year. Always telling Owen he wasn't going anywhere.

His husband-to-be cleaned up well. Not that he didn't always look great in his suits. Harrison's face lit up when he noticed Owen staring at him. Owen smiled back. This was it. Today was the day he was going to pledge himself to Harrison for the rest of his life. He was more ready now than he'd ever been.

They had decided to do their own vows. It was nerve racking trying to figure out what he wanted to say. He hated being put on the spot, so he'd spent most of the month leading up to the wedding working on what he'd say. Owen hadn't been the only one. He'd walked in on Harrison a couple times when he was working on his vows. It had been funny to watch him slam his computer shut and glare at him until he left. He couldn't wait to hear what Harrison would say.

Owen walked over to Harrison and took his hands. "Ready?"

"Yep." His soon-to-be husband nodded.

"Nervous?" Owen squeezed Harrison's hands.

"Nope." He didn't look away from Owen.

It was a special moment.

"Whatever. I had to drag him here because he kept checking himself out in the mirror. If he wasn't messing with his hair, he was 'fixing' his tie." Mac snorted.

At least until Mac put his two cents in.

"Uncle Owen was the same way!" His niece shook her head.

"Give a guy a break." He lunged at Gabbi. She shrieked and darted behind her mom.

"I think everyone is in there. They are just waiting for the two of you. Gabbi, you want to go first or second?" Mac was taking charge.

It was a good thing someone was or Owen would just stand there, looking at Harrison.

"You go first." Gabbi bit her lip.

It seemed she was the nervous one.

Mac opened the door and nodded to someone. Music started and he walked in. Gabbi waited a few seconds before following. Susan had gone inside as soon as they'd arrived. It was just him and Harrison standing by the door, getting ready for the rest of their lives. It was more than Owen could ever hope for. He was happy he'd finally found the one meant for him. The guy his mom told him would be there for him when he was ready. He missed her, but she was here in spirit. It was all he could hope for. Owen knew she'd be happy for him because that was all she'd ever wanted — for her children to be happy with the life they had, not to wish for something out of reach.

It might have taken a tragedy to bring them together, but it would be happy sailing from here on out. Well, maybe not too happy, a bumpy ride could be fun. He heard makeup sex was great. So far, he hadn't had a chance to experience it, but life couldn't always be sunshine and roses.

But today? Today was going to be the best day of his life.

* * * *

The ceremony was over in a blur of vows and Elvis singing. Harrison wanted to remember every detail. Good thing they'd opted to have it videotaped. The pictures had been fun. Elvis was in a couple. They got some shots by the gazebo too. People might think getting married at an Elvis chapel was cheesy, but it had been fun. Something they would look back on and smile. Seeing everyone dance out of the place had been one of the highlights. Mac getting down to Elvis had been spectacular.

They didn't need something expensive and traditional. This was perfect for the two of them. Harrison found Owen had a wonderful sense of humor. Harrison did have to put his foot down on the Hawaiian shirt idea. He'd been all for fun, but he wanted to be dressed up for his wedding. It was a special day and seeing Owen in a tux had been worth it. The man was too stunning for his own good and he was all Harrison's.

Owen was driving them back to their place. Susan had everything set up last night so they just had to put the cake out with a few munchies. He figured most people wouldn't stay long. If they did, Susan would have to lock up because he was taking Owen to the Totally Five Star and having his way with him.

Last night had been brutal. He'd gotten so used to sleeping with Owen it was hard to fall asleep without him there. They pulled into the driveway. There was nowhere else to go with all of the cars up and down the street. There were so many it almost looked like a parking lot. Susan and Gabbi were already there. Owen took off his seatbelt and moved so he was facing Harrison.

"Husband."

"Yes, husband?" Harrison was going to have a hard time getting that stupid grin off of his face.

"I just wanted to say it." Owen leaned over and brushed his lips against Harrison's. "How about we ditch this sideshow and head to the hotel?" Owen swiped his thumb over Harrison's lips, like he was rubbing the kiss in somehow.

"You know your sister wants pictures of me stuffing cake in your face. She said that was the best part of getting married."

"She would." Owen chuckled.

"Okay, here's the plan. Go in. Say his. Dance to some song your sister picked out. Cut the cake. Say goodbye. An hour tops. Two if we have to. Then we are off to the suite."

"I can do that. Maybe. I need another kiss to hold me over." This time Owen did more than brush their lips together, he licked Harrison's lips requesting entry and he couldn't deny Owen anything.

A knock on the window startled them both into ending the kiss.

"Come one, Uncle Harrison, stop making kissy face with Uncle Owen. We have a cake to cut." Gabbi glared in at them, her arms across her chest like she meant business.

Harrison had known she was going to wear the tux, but he wasn't prepared for how dashing she looked. They were going to have to beat suitors off her with a stick. And he was happy to say he was looking forward to that part of being an uncle. He was very protective of Gabbi. Almost as if she was his kid. God, what would he do if *they* had kids of their own?

That was something to think about another time. Not right now. But—kids. As freaked as he might be, he thought Owen would make a wonderful dad. He'd seen how he was with Gabbi. Hell, with his sister and mom too. One of the many reasons he loved his husband.

They walked into the house to applause and people whistling. Owen waved so Harrison followed suit. What else could he do? Everyone was so happy. It was well deserved. Not just for him and Owen, but for everyone who'd been put through hell because of Raymond. They'd invited Jade and Tommy. He noticed them over by the cake with Gabbi. The two kids seemed to hit it off.

Susan walked through the room, handing everyone champagne.

"A toast. I know Gabbi is the best man and I'm sure she has something she wants to say, but I want to start. Owen. You have always been there for me no matter how bad I screwed up. And I did. Screw up. A lot. Earlier this year, you literally saved my life with the help of your handsome husband, Harrison. If not for the two of you, I wouldn't be able to watch my wonderful daughter grow up. So thank you. And I want to wish the two of you the happiest of lives. You both deserve the world and I know you'll give it to each other!" Susan raised her glass and took a drink.

Owen had tears in his eyes, but so did Harrison. Susan had grown so much since the kidnapping. He was proud of her.

"I'm next! Thank you, Uncle Harrison, for coming into Uncle Owen's life. He needed you. Bad." Gabbi had to pause because the small crowd laughed. "I am happy I get to call you uncle. Uncle Owen. Like Mom said, you've always been there and I love you so much. I'm happy that you're so happy. Harrison is good for you. He's a keeper." Gabbi raised her glass and took a sip. She wrinkled her nose and handed it off to her mom. "And champagne is gross."

There was more laughter. A few more people toasted before it was time for the cake. It was almost too pretty to cut. Three tiers with roses. All white. The topper was two men kissing with Mr. and Mr. behind them. Susan handed him a knife. He looked down at it.

"What am I supposed to do with this?"

"You and Owen both cut into the cake. Get a piece that is big enough for both of you. Feed each other, then I'll get everyone else some cake."

"We got this, Harrison." Owen sounded so confident.

Harrison handed over the knife.

Owen placed it against the cake and tugged Harrison closer so he could grip his hand over Owen's. It was fairly easy. It was a small piece. Owen took half of it in his hands and put it against Harrison's lips. He opened up, not sure if Owen was going to be nice or not. It was good cake. He licked the icing off Owen's finger before taking his piece. Since Owen was nice, he followed suit. He wasn't expecting Gabbi to come up and smear icing in both of their faces when they were going in for a kiss.

"You can get enough of that later." Gabbi stood with her hands on her hips. She smiled when people laughed. Gabbi was enjoying the spotlight.

Owen chased her around the table and out of the door.

"Sometimes I wonder who is older." Susan came to stand beside him.

"Gabbi for sure." Harrison laughed.

* * * *

Things were winding down. They'd been there more than the two hours they'd planned, but it was fun talking to all of their friends and just enjoying the party. Now it was time to go. Harrison went and rounded up Owen. He was slightly tipsy and loose. Harrison had never seen him this way. Susan ushered them out the door, assuring them she'd pack up and their place would be nice and clean when they returned.

It was a good thing Harrison had stuck with the one glass or they'd have to call a cab.

"I love you." Owen gave Harrison a sloppy kiss on the cheek.

"I love you too, baby."

"Thanks for marrying me."

"I'd do it all over again in a heartbeat."

"Aww. That makes me love you more." Owen patted Harrison's face.

Harrison helped Owen into the car and made sure his belt was buckled. He hurried to the driver side. The ride to the hotel was over quickly. Owen kept himself amused by messing with the radio and Harrison watched the beautiful scenery. He loved Vegas at night. All lit up.

He handed the keys off to the valet. Harrison didn't want to have to worry about finding a spot. He tipped the guy and led Owen to the elevator. He'd gotten the key last night and their bags for the weekend were already there.

"Good evening, Mr. Boone. Congratulations."

"Thank you." He smiled at the group by the front desk. Working in the hotel was like living in a small town. Everyone knew everything.

Owen waved. The elevator dinged and Harrison hurried Owen inside. Once the doors closed, Owen wrapped himself around Harrison.

"We're all alone now." Owen placed kisses wherever he could reach on Harrison.

He would laugh if he wasn't so horny.

"At last."

"Hmm. I can't wait to get you naked." Owen slid his hand down Harrison's body and grabbed his cock through the tuxedo pants.

"As much as I would love to get naked right here, we should wait for the room. Cameras." Harrison pointed up.

"Hi!" Owen grinned and waved.

Owen was fun tipsy. Harrison managed to get them to the room. Who would have thought a major crime would bring the two men together? Harrison never thought he'd be so lucky to have Owen in his life. He was going to do everything in his power to make his husband the happiest man on Earth.

He fiddled with the lock and Owen pushed the doors open. He moved into the room, taking his pants off as he went.

"Come claim me, Mr. Boone."

Harrison shut the door and started the first day of the rest of his life — with the man he loved. He couldn't ask for anything more. Except maybe kids. He'd bring that up in the morning.

About the Author

Jambrea wanted to be the youngest romance author published, but life impeded the dreams. She put her writing aside and went to college briefly, then enlisted in the Air Force. After serving in the military, she returned home to Indiana to start her family. A few years later, she discovered yahoo groups and book reviews. There was no turning back. She was bit by the writing bug.

She enjoys spending time with her son when not writing and loves to receive reader feedback. She's addicted to the internet so feel free to email her anytime.

Jambrea Jo Jones loves to hear from readers. You can find her contact information, website and author biography at http://pride-publishing.com.

PUBLISHING